Money makes people do terrible things.

"Stanley, please call the police," Rebecca asked as they reached Aunt Bernice's room.

"Certainly." Stanley turned and walked downstairs.

"What are you doing? Stop that. You can't break into her safe." Shouts of indignation were erupting from the bedroom. Rebecca and Rupert rushed into the room to find the doctor wrestling with a woman in her thirties.

"All right, that's enough. Kirsch, let the doctor go!" Rebecca shouted. They immediately stopped their struggling, staring incredulously at the new arrivals.

Rebecca moved toward them but Rupert grabbed her shoulder and pulled her back behind him. Then she noticed the black pistol in Kirsch's hand.

"What the hell do you think you're doing?" Rebecca stepped around Rupert. "Drop that gun before you hurt yourself."

"I know how to use this." Waving the gun at them, Miss Kirsch stepped away from the doctor lying on the floor. "I'm defending what belonged to Mrs. Simmons. I'm not going to let this man steal her things."

MOSAIC

Rita Schulz

53rd Street Publishing
Head office: Gibsons B.C. Canada
www.53rdsteetpublishing.com

53RD STREET PUBLISHING

Mosaic
Rita Schulz

Published by 53rd Street Publishing
Copyright 2016 Rita Schulz

Cover art © Can Stock Photo Inc. / Vertyr
Cover designed by R. Edgewood
Cover design and layout copyright 2016 by 53rd Street Publishing
ISBN 978-1-927621-54-7

53rd Street Publishing
Head office: Gibsons B.C. Canada
www.53rdsteetpublishing.com

Other Collections by Rita Schulz

Fantastic Five
Ten Tempting Tales
The Dark Zone
Unique Tales of the Fantastic
Tales of the Fantastic

With R.S. Meger
The Fantastic Five

With Russ Crossley
Ladies of the Jolly Roger
The Reckoning

With Russ Crossley and R.G. Hart
Nightmares

Table of Contents

Dedication

For my family and friends on the Sunshine Coast.

Introduction

When you read a lot of short fiction unique voices always stand above the rest. Rita Schulz is one such voice.

Some would describe her style as gentle; I would describe it as a luxurious read on a sea of story. She has the ability to tell even the most on the edge of your seat story in such a way as to be lulled into a false sense of security then a surprise twist shocks the reader like a rubber band being suddenly snapped.

This collection is not one genre of fiction. It is intended to be a cross section of different genres designed to explore the range of storytelling by the extraordinary writer.

We have selected these stories ranging from horror, to mystery, to science fiction and fantasy to young adult for you the reader to enjoy.

After you complete this incredible journey look for forthcoming novels from Rita. They'll be ones you won't want to miss.

R. Edgewood
Managing Editor
53rd Street Publishing

The Prize

In a steampunk London a desperate young woman struggles to escape a life of poverty. What she discovers is life can indeed be its own reward.

THE FIRE IN THE old black woodstove would be going out soon. The smell of dust and rot was everywhere. Soon I would hear Mother call for me to get more wood. It would be easier if I just got it now. Why did I wait?

It was a cold winter and it seemed Bromley, an outer borough of London, was especially hard hit with snow. My stomach ached with hunger. I can't remember the last time I had a full meal.

I drew my limbs close to my body to gain warmth but it didn't help; I still shivered. The fire was so small it hardly threw any heat into the kitchen. My bare feet were cold; it felt like they were freezing solid to our hard, dirt floor. I pulled my dark gray shawl closer around my shoulders. Getting up, I went outside to bring in a few pieces of precious wood. I would put water on the stovetop to boil. It would be nice to have hot water this morning. Mother would like that.

I looked toward the cot where Mother lay huddled under the blankets. She hadn't moved very much last night, and not at all this morning, but at least her coughing had stopped.

1

The Prize

There were only the two of us; we depended on each other.

I got up—my arms and legs were blue—and drew back the flimsy pine door. The cold wind hit me in the face and I shivered. Immediately my breath turned to clouds of fog. I raced around the corner of the house to the woodpile to grab a few pieces of wood and bring them inside.

By the time I slammed the door shut, my teeth were chattering and my hands were white. I dropped two of the pieces of wood in the stove and used a long wooden stick to shift the still warm embers inside. The wood caught quickly. The water bucket next to the stove was half full, so I poured some into our battered kettle on the stove to heat water.

I finally tried to wake up Mother. She didn't move or breathe. She was dead.

I felt a rushing noise in my ears as my heart hammered hard. *What do I do now?* I started to cry. I cried so hard I thought I was going to throw up, but I couldn't stop. I loved my mother. I wanted her to come back to me.

Mother told me I didn't have a father—that she had made a mistake when she was young, but she wouldn't ask for help or forgiveness from her family. She said they were dead to her and to me. She never spoke of them again.

I understood what pride was. I also understood I was an orphan at eight years old.

I had to find someplace to live. I had to keep out of the orphanages—you disappeared once you got sent to an orphanage.

I went through the wicker basket mother kept under the bed next to her shoes. It had a heavy shawl and the one good dress mother wore to church.

The dress didn't fit me, but I took the shawl and used bits of rags to stuff in her shoes so I could wear them.

On the bottom of the basket, I found something beautiful. It was a necklace with a round, gleaming black stone. It was smooth, though rough in spots with flecks of gold and silver, hanging off the end of a long black cord. I slipped it around my neck and felt it grow warm against my skin.

There were a couple of shillings in a small cloth bag in her purse, nothing else. I searched everywhere.

I knew that I had to get away from where we lived. I thought it would be best if I went to London. I'd heard of London, a big city with lots of fancy people. *I could find a place to live there.*

***

I laughed as I adjusted my driving goggles with their amber-tinted lenses. My best friend, Elizabeth Sutton, had come by with her new steam automobile. She let me drive. Yes, I was driving a steam automobile!

It was a beautiful blue, sunny morning and Elizabeth, a very pretty girl with a round face, dark hair, and rosebud lips, had just gotten a new black steam automobile for doing well in finishing school. The air flowing over me was fresh with the smell of new mown grass and roses.

I wondered what the rich people were doing. It would have been grand if Queen Victoria could see us. If Her Highness could only see women and men driving these silly, noisy, wonderful machines…but she was taking care of government. I wondered if she ever got out and had any fun?

Elizabeth and I were both sixteen at a time where wonderful things were happening: steam automobiles, women free to vote, and magic that was real. Alchemy was the newest popular topic on everyone's lips. We attended a talk and demonstration on alchemy only last week.

Today I planned that I would go back to Bromley to visit the place I grew up and where I lived until I was eight years old. I had unanswered questions and needed to find answers.

I needed to find out who I was—not just Annabelle Combs, a name my mother called me.

Did I have any family? Mother said they were dead to her, but that didn't mean they had died. Then there was my pendant. The more I learned about alchemy, the more I thought the stone in the pendant could be a Philosopher's Stone, something sorcerers use to cast magic spells.

My mind shied away from the very idea I could have anything to do with magic, but at the same time, I was filled with excitement.

Thankfully Elizabeth showed up with her new steam mobile to distract me.

"Elizabeth, this is really too much fun," I said when I pulled to the side of the road with a quick jerk of the steering wheel. The steam vehicle bumped into the curb as it came to a stop.

"Good job, Annabelle, that was a first-rate effort for your first time driving," said Elizabeth as she laughed.

"I'm still not sure about Elizabeth and Annabelle. It feels so formal, so strange," I said to her. We had been raised almost as sisters, and using our full first names rather than our nicknames was a new formality for us.

My aunt, Mrs. Timmons, had been the nanny to Elizabeth and her younger brother Matthew, the Sutton children.

In truth, Mrs. Timmons was no relation to me at all. She had found me when she had taken her wards, Elizabeth and Mathew, to the park. I had just arrived in London and had seen a lovely park. I went over to watch the children play. I noticed a man striding toward me wearing a long black coat and hat.

"What are you doing here and who are you with, little girl?" he asked in a deep, menacing voice.

I started shaking; I couldn't speak. I knew that this must be the man from the orphanage. He was here to get me. I looked up and saw a woman hurrying over to us. She reached over to me and took my hand.

"My name is Mrs. Timmons and I'd like to know what you're doing with my niece?" she said as she started fussing with my dress, trying to wipe off the dirt with her gloves.

"Trust me. What's your name?" she whispered in my ear.

"Elizabeth," I whispered back.

"Excuse me. I was told there was a homeless girl in the park and I've come to pick her up," said the man. He was looking around the park with a scowl on his face.

"Oh, my. What have you done to your dress? Disgusting. Were you playing in the brambles by the stream again? I told you not to go that far. Come on home; we've got to give you a good scrubbing and change your clothes.

"You'll have to try somewhere else. I don't see any child that fits that description," Mrs. Timmons said to the man as she turned her back on him and led me back to where her two charges were waiting.

As of that day, Mrs. Timmons and her husband became my family. They had no children of their own and had always wanted a little girl. I told them my mother had died that morning and that I left and came to London to hide from the orphanage.

She told me that when she was a child, she was almost sent to an orphanage too. I was told to call them Aunt Kerry and Uncle Burt. No one knew the truth of our relationship except the three of us. They never asked any more about where I came from or about my family. Even when Aunt Kerry saw my necklace, she touched it but didn't say anything.

Today I needed to go home. I'd been feeling the need for a while; it had been building and today was the day I'd go back to that cold, dirty shack.

"That was wonderful, Beth. I hope I can still call you Beth when we're alone."

We came from different classes in society. Beth grew up an aristocrat, the Suttons of the Thames, Left Bank, and I did not.

"Of course, you silly goose. Where are you going now?"

"I want to go to Bromley, take a look around, then come back. I'm looking for placement. I saw a notice on the job posting board that an estate in Bromley is hiring for a nanny. I don't think Bromley would be suitable for me, but I thought I'd give the town a quick look." I left it at that. My words had a little truth to them.

"Why not drive?"

"Oh, no, I couldn't." My heart beat hard as I thought of her visiting the slum where I spent my childhood.

"Look, I will take you to Bromley," Beth offered as she stepped out the passenger door of the vehicle.

"It's in the country and has a little village; let's explore. If it's not to our liking, we can leave. It will be good driving practice for me. We'll stop at home and tell Mother."

I began to calm down as I considered Beth's plan. It would be nice to go for a drive. My pendant grew warm against my skin after my decision, telling me I'd made the right one.

***

Soon I was on the road, seated next to Beth in the passenger seat. It was a lovely sunny day with only a few light clouds in the sky. The warm spring wind whipped my fine blonde hair into my face. It was so much fun. Every time we came to a bump in the road, it was like we left the ground and flew.

Deep down I knew that this was a mistake, taking Beth with me, but I couldn't resist. I told myself that if I didn't get the answers I needed today, then I would go back another time and talk to the people who lived there when I did. Maybe someone remembered me and my mother.

We arrived in Bromley and took a driving tour of the town. It didn't take long; it was only one muddy road with a few dirty shops with peeling paint and boarded-up windows. It seemed a poorer town now than when I lived here. *Was that possible?*

"Beth, could I drive a little?"

Beth smiled and nodded. We switched places and soon I was heading down a lane barely wide enough to accommodate the steam mobile. Finally the road narrowed so much I had to stop and pull over. Luckily it was very close to my ultimate destination, my old home.

"Beth, I need to check something out. Why don't you stay here and wait for me. I won't be long. I don't want you to get your boots all muddy." My stomach was tied in knots. *Please don't ask any questions.* Thankfully she nodded. It seemed she understood my need for privacy.

I walked down the narrow lane leading to an overgrown footpath to where our shack had once stood.

It was gone, everything was gone. There were no boards or bricks left to show that there had ever been a small home there.

It was an open field, a pasture, and now part of a farm. I knew rural areas like Bromley were called upon to produce more food for London because the city was growing so quickly. I spotted a familiar house, but it had been a long way from ours when I was young. I didn't have much time, so I rushed to the front porch of the house and knocked on the door.

After a few moments, the door opened and there stood an older woman with two children. A small blonde child was cradled in the woman's arms and the other peeked out from behind her dress, staring at me with coal black eyes.

Oh God. It took me a moment to realize this wasn't an older woman, it was Mandy, a girl I knew from down the lane. *She's my age.*

"Hello. My name is Bella and I used to live down the lane."

"I remember you and your mum," said Mandy, staring at me. "You've done all right for yourself, haven't you? "

"A kind couple took me in." I didn't want to answerer any questions. I was here to get information, not give it.

"What do you want? When your mum died and you were gone too, we got the land. You can't have it back, we bought it."

I was in shock, my stomach started to heave. My life would be like Mandy's if I had been taken to the orphanage. The baby started to fuss and Mandy started to close the door.

"No, I'm not interested in the land. I've come to find my mum. Where was she buried?" I quickly asked.

"In a pauper's grave. No one paid for her burial and no one came to mourn for her. Check with the church up the hill."

I knew the church and the nearby graveyard. Everyone who couldn't afford their own grave, and pay the church to bury them, was buried in an unmarked grave outside hallowed or blessed ground.

"Has anyone asked about us? Anyone?"

Mandy opened the door and stared at me with her head tilted slightly to one side with her eyes narrowed to slits. "No, why would someone come for you? What have you done?"

My mind raced. I had hoped that maybe a member of my family had come to find us, or to grieve Mother's passing. No one. *There is no one and nothing here for me.* I fished around in the bottom of my purse and pulled out a shilling, which I handed to her, then I stepped back from her door.

"Thank you for taking the time, Mandy. I hope all goes well for you and your family."

Mandy snatched the coin out of my hand like it was solid gold, then slammed the door in my face.

I turned and hurried to where I had left Beth in the steam mobile. There was no need to come back here ever again. I would send a tithe to the church to light a candle and ask them to say prayers for my mother. Then my responsibilities were done.

***

I loved the new watch Aunt Kerry and Uncle Burt had given me. It was beautiful. Large and full of working dials and springs, the watch even told the time. I had done well in my studies too and had taken firsts in all my classes.

I had decided to become a nanny.

The education was very good. I learned deportment, languages, cooking, and how to run a household.

I checked my watch again. I didn't want to be late, but I didn't want to show up too early either, for fear I'd appear too desperate. I wanted to be a few minutes early, which meant being punctual in my book.

I'd been gathering information for the past year, in the newspaper and word-of-mouth, about nanny positions and households that had large libraries. I wanted to learn more about alchemy. It was a topic that fascinated me, so I would need access to books. The only way I could get hold of the books was to buy them or work in a household where I could use or borrow them.

I think that I may have found a good match with the Langdon's. They have a son who married two years ago; his wife recently gave birth to a child. There was a notice in the newspapers that the Langdon's were looking for a nanny or governess. With my training, I qualified for either position.

To make sure I got the job, I had written up a very fine letter of reference from the Suttons. I thought the signature was very well done. I practiced the flow of Mrs. Sutton's writing style until it looked perfect. I copied it from the Christmas card they gave Aunt Kerry last year. Unethical, perhaps a little, but I needed everything to go without a hitch so I couldn't take a chance on a less than stellar reference letter.

I had butterflies fluttering in the pit of my stomach and my knees wanted to knock together. I took in a deep breath. *What's the worst that can happen?* They might say no. If they did, then fine, I could live with their decision no matter the outcome. I had other options but this really seemed like the best one.

I stood by the servant's door, exhaled, and knocked. I put my pleasant face on and waited. I thought that if I could get this position, it would serve two purposes: I would get a well-paying job, and most importantly, I would have access to Mr. Edmond Langdon's library. It was said that he had thousands of books on all kinds of topics. But what he was known for was his collection of alchemy books. That's what I wanted—no, needed—to learn.

A young lady dressed in a black-and-white maid's uniform answered the door.

"I'm here to see Mrs. Langdon for the nanny position. I have an appointment," I explained.

"That's fine, Miss, please come with me. I'll take you to the day room, then call Mrs. Langdon."

We walked through the kitchen, with its smell of warm baked bread and crisp bacon, down the walnut-paneled hall to the day room.

The day room was bright. Sunlight streamed through the tall windows overlooking the garden beyond. The room was painted a cheerful yellow, and sheer white curtains bordered the windows. There was an azure vase filled with an assortment of fragrant spring flowers between two leather wing chairs, and a matching couch.

The interview went well with Mrs. Langdon, senior, who then called for her daughter-in-law to join us with the child.

Oh, dear. I hadn't prepared myself to meet the child so soon. They can be so frightening and unreasonable at times.

"What a lovely child." I reached out to take the child that was being thrust toward me. The little darling was sleeping. When it woke for a moment, it just drooled and went back to sleep.

"How long have you taken care of children?" asked young Mrs. Langdon.

"I've done the interview," interrupted senior Mrs. Langdon before I could respond. "She's more than suitable. I just wanted you and Maxwell to meet her before I hired her."

The tension in my body eased at Mrs. Langdon's words of confidence in me. I smiled for the first time since the interview started. Now I needed to determine my working hours and my salary.

"Yes, Mother Langdon. Maxwell seems to like her. He didn't make the slightest fuss when she held him," said the younger Mrs. Langdon.

Mrs. Langdon outlined my duties, which were reasonable, and offered a generous salary. I was pleased.

"Well, what do you say? When would you be able to start?" the senior Mrs. Langdon asked me.

"When would you need me?"

"As soon as possible would be wonderful," said the mother of Maxwell, her large blue eyes shining with hope.

I thought of how long it would take for me to say good-bye to Aunt Kerry and Uncle Burt, and of course Beth, Matt, and their family. I had to pack my clothes, a few hats, but if Beth would give me a ride in her steam automobile, it wouldn't take long at all.

"I would say Monday?"

"Oh, that long?" asked the mother, her eyes losing some of their shine and her lips developing a pout.

I thought of the library. The sooner I was living here, the sooner I could start my real education in alchemy. My necklace grew warm on my skin, telling me it seemed to agree with me.

"I finished school and am between appointments at the moment. I could possibly start Friday?" I volunteered.

"If you start on Thursday, in two days, I will give you a bonus," said the young woman, naming a generous amount.

12

It was like she was playing cards and just slapped down the winning hand. She watched me, her eyes calm and calculating.

I wonder who is playing whom?

"Very well. If I make the arrangements quickly, I might be able to do it." I nodded as I pretended to think. "Fine. I will start this Thursday."

We stood simultaneously and I was shown out the servant's door off the kitchen. I walked down the street, struggling to contain my excitement. Once around the corner, out of sight of the Langford residence, I stopped.

"I did it!" I shouted, not caring who heard me. It was then that I realized that I hadn't given senior Mrs. Langdon my reference letter. A large amount of stress lifted from my shoulders as I closed my eyes in relief.

***

My family and friends understood and were pleased for me.

The time went quickly at the Langdon's'.

As I expected, in the evenings I had time to myself to study after Maxwell went down for the night.

Upon arriving, the first thing I did was to put Maxwell on a regular schedule rather than letting him do what he wanted. It was hard for him for the first two weeks, but I persevered and made his doting mother and grandmother listen to me. After that it was smooth sailing and Master Maxwell turned out to be a delightful child.

After a couple of years, it was time to move on.

Finally the day came to resign and leave being a nanny and governess and follow my goal of being an alchemist.

"Mrs. Langdon," I said, addressing both ladies in the day room. "I asked you here this afternoon to let you know I plan on continuing my education. I will be leaving your employment at the end of the month."

Both women gasped at me in shock and looked at each other.

"I know you're sure of your decision, but Annabelle, you will be so missed. Not just with your diligence and care of Maxwell, but your help in everything on the estate," said Mrs. Langdon senior.

"Please don't go," said young Mrs. Langdon, her eyes filling with tears.

"You'll all be fine without me." As I said these words, I knew they would be fine. We'd learned a lot from each other in my time here.

***

I had seen an advertisement in the paper for a job I couldn't pass up. It was for an alchemist's apprentice, posted by a very well-known alchemist, Alex Collins. He had even preformed successfully before Queen Victoria. I needed to work with him.

I was pleased to find his office was in a respectable area of the city, on the edge of London's business district. I had written to Master Collins for an appointment and received an answer. Not quite as hopeful an answer as I wished, but it seemed the position was still available and he was still interviewing.

I decided to spend a little of my precious money and hire a steam automobile. This way I would arrive quickly and not be too tired. I wanted to be fresh for the interview.

Once at Master Collins' office, I stepped out of the steam mobile, adjusted my new goggles with rose-colored lenses, and straightened my short burgundy riding jacket.

The street reeked of steam, horses, and mud. Not very pleasant, but that was what big cities were like.

My nerves danced in my gut. I thought I would throw up my meager breakfast before long. I fought back the bile that crept up in the back of my throat.

Once outside the office, I knocked on the door, trying to hide my trembling hands by gripping my purse and thinking calming thoughts.

If this didn't work out, what was the worst that could happen? Oh, yes, of course. I would merely be penniless and homeless on the street. The scenario of this nightmare that I had grown up with is one I still wake up from in the middle of the night.

The door opened and there stood a young boy, who I estimated was about eight years of age. He had light brown hair, big gray eyes, and a dimple on his right cheek.

"Hello," he said with a friendly, cheery voice.

"Hello. I'm here to see Master Collins. I'm—"

"Annabelle Combs," he finished for me. "Yes, I know. Come this way, Miss."

What an impertinent imp—but smart, very smart.

He turned, left the door open, then ran up the staircase to the floors above the reception area, his small steps thumping, echoing in the confined space. My necklace started warming against my skin. I followed him.

The hall and stairs were in warm tones of oak. It looked like it had been freshly polished and the sunlight coming through the front windows around the door shone on the wood, adding to the cozy feeling.

I managed to get to the top of the staircase just in time to see the young lad run into the first door to the right.

Breathing hard from the sudden exertion, I knocked on the doorframe, having decided not to enter unannounced. No answer.

"Hello, is there anyone here?" I called.

"Yes. Rudy, bring our visitor to my office," said a muffled yet mellow sounding man's voice from somewhere in the room beyond the doorway.

"Yes, sir." This was followed by footsteps, and a head popped around the doorframe in front of me.

"Come on, then," said the lad as he reached forward, grabbed my hand, and pulled me into a room. Then let go. It looked like a reception room, with basic small desk and waiting chairs along one side.

The lad stopped and shook his head, then grabbed my hand again and led me through another door into an inner office.

Behind a plain pine desk piled high with papers sat a slender man of medium height. He had swept-back short hair and was clean-shaven. Next to him on the wall was a wooden bookcase filled with books, and on the top, every inch of space contained what looked like ordinary rocks of every shape, size, and color. The windowsills were filled with crystals. Sunlight shining through and off the crystals filled the room with rainbows of colors.

"Rudy, you may un-hand Miss Combs and leave us alone," said the man, regarding me with an amused expression on his lean features. He leaned forward and interlocked his long slender fingers.

"Please sit down, Miss Combs. I am Alex Collins. I understand you are here for the interview for an alchemist apprentice? My apprentice, perhaps?"

"Yes, sir, I am." I stopped talking and waited. If this was Master Collins, then he looked like an ordinary man, dressed in a dark, three-piece gray suit and a crisp white shirt.

Master Collins unfolded his fingers, then, with the fingers of his right hand, he reached underneath his shirt collar and pulled out a necklace the twin of mine and smiled.

"Welcome, Belle. I'm so glad you decided to join me." His voice had taken on a higher, warm, friendly tone.

I sat speechless but managed to pull out my necklace too. Now I recognized his voice. A voice from my past.

"Mother?" I sat dazed, staring at a woman I thought dead. My mind whirled with questions.

"What? How? You died. I was told you were buried in a pauper's grave. I went back. The shack, everything is gone." My mind started to whirl, I felt the sound around me dampen as if everything was far away. I blinked hard and squeezed my fingers together and my nails gouged into my palms. I focused on the pain.

"Yes, you're right, my darling daughter. I need to explain a few things. Please give me some time, then, if you still have questions, I'll answer them as best I can. Of course, the job is yours if you're still interested."

"Thank you." I responded automatically, still trying to make sense of her words. The job was mine. My mother was alive. She was sitting in front of me, dressed as a man.

My stomach tightened and anger welled from within me. "You left me all alone. I grieved for you. I was terrified. I almost ended up in an orphanage. How could you do that to a small child! Your only daughter!" My voice had been rising until now I was shouting. My whole body shook so hard and I couldn't stop it.

Sudden calming warmth came from my chest, growing stronger with each second. I needed to calm down. I focused on the warmth, then the kaleidoscope of colors on the wall created by the crystals.

My mother softly and slowly began to explain.

"For starters, I have always been there for you, but you didn't know it. I had magic, so it wasn't hard to slow down my heart to make it appear I was dead. I had already taken a few trips into town and started performing magic and had some money saved up. At the time, there was a young woman from a poor family who died who resembled me, so I purchased her body from the family for a small sum."

"They needed money to survive over the winter and I arranged for the husband to start a new job far from Bromley the following spring.

"When you left Bromley, that kind woman you spoke to and joined on the trip to London was paid to accompany you to the park. Mrs. Timmons was hired by me to meet you by the park and take care of you for the next eight years. I always knew what you were doing and where you were. I even saw you occasionally. I left nothing to chance. My fame and fortune followed quickly directly in relation to how hard I worked and my own magic.."

As I heard the words, I felt myself beginning to calm down. She-he, my mother, spoke in a quiet, dispassionate voice that helped steady me. I listen carefully to each word she spoke.

"I had to work on my own gifts, goals, and career. It's a man's world and I am under constant scrutiny by the public. At the time I couldn't have a child with me. I had to wait until you were old enough to join me. Do you understand?" she asked at last.

I didn't trust myself to answer yet. The warmth coming from my necklace was increasing. I felt surrounded by wellbeing.

"I know it will take a while for you to understand completely. All I ask is that you forgive me. Perhaps not now, but maybe later as you learn more about your gifts and our life."

I met her eyes and nodded dumbly. I was in shock. I knew that anger and other emotions would follow.

"Daughter, will you stay and receive your inheritance, the prize of becoming a great alchemist?"

I swallowed hard, but there was only one answer I could possibly give. "Yes, I will accept. Teach me."

Anna's Dream

A teenage girl fears her dreams for her future are about to be dashed when an unexpected ally enters her life.

ANNA LOOKED DOWN at the thin white paper that was her class schedule for this year and gripped it tightly in her shaking fingers. She'd have to put it into her backpack before she ruined it.

She had done it, she had put down art as her elective. Her stomach was in knots. If her parents knew, they'd make her change it and then ground her for a year.

Walking with short, fast steps, she made her way down the crowded gray hallways. Her nose wrinkled. The hallway smelled of unwashed bodies and floor cleaner. She hurried toward the cafeteria where she would meet her best friends, Ellen and Beverly, for lunch.

She was excited and nervous. It was exciting to finally be in high school, grade nine; and getting to pick out a course you really want was thrilling and nerve-racking at the same time. Choosing your classes was a big decision, one that could alter the course of her life. Okay, that was a little over the top, but that's what it meant to her.

Anna kept her eyes on the yellow-and-red tiled floor as she walked. The tiles always reminded her of random splatters of mustard and catsup—or worse, dried blood. Horrible.

For a moment she thought about going to her locker to get her books for this afternoon's classes, but she might run into Roger Klassen, the boy with the locker next to hers.

He insisted on slamming his locker door into hers whenever she was there, so going to her locker wasn't high on her must-do list right now.

Looking down the hallway, she checked the time on the office clock. She had to get to the cafeteria quickly; the school was getting so full of new students, sometimes it was hard to find a place to sit. She really hoped Beverly and Ellen had gotten their usual table.

She and Ellen had been best friends all the way through elementary school and had spent most of their recesses and lunch periods together. Over the years, they'd even had a few classes and homerooms together. Beverly had joined them in third grade after moving into the South Vancouver area.

Anna entered the dimly lit cafeteria and had to squint to see the back wall. It didn't matter how many lights this large area had, it was always dim. The light just seemed to disappear into the ceiling. She peered at the ceiling. Sure enough, the lights were on, but it always took her eyes a couple of minutes to adjust to the gloom.

She made her way in the direction of the table where she and her friends usually sat, while looking around trying to see if they had moved to another table.

"Anna, here we are," said a small voice beside her hip. Looking down, Anna saw Ellen; she had a big smile on her face and a twinkle in her large brown eyes.

"It was approved. I'm going to take art this year," said Anna in a singsong voice as she threw one leg over the bench-style table seat and sat down. She hated these stupid beige Arborite picnic bench tables. They were all one piece, the table and the benches, so you had to lift your leg up and over the long chair portion. How awkward.

21

Especially with Anna's short legs, it was always embarrassing for her. Good thing she usually wore slacks to school.

"What are your parents going to say?" asked Ellen. She knew Anna's parents, so the question was a good one.

Anna shrugged, pulled out the salami sandwich her mother had made for her, took a bite, and swallowed. "Mom and Dad won't say anything. It's been approved by the office."

Beverly shook her head, her deep blue eyes blinked like an owl behind her thick round glasses. "Your parents have to sign the form. Only then can you hand it in to the office. And only then can you take the class."

Anna's sandwich hit the pit of her stomach, then tried to immediately come back up. She wasn't counting on her parents finding out until after midterms. She thought once the interim marks came out, then she could show her parents how well she was doing and they'd let her stay in the art class she really, really wanted.

This was horrible, a complete disaster. *No way, Beverly must be wrong.* But Ellen was nodding her head in agreement as she bit into her apple.

"So you agree with me, right, Ellen?" Anna had the feeling she was grasping for straws, but she was trying to hold on to her hopes.

Ellen mumbled around the apple chunk but her words were unmistakable. "No, Anna, sorry, but Beverly is right." She swallowed, then added, "Actually, you're both right, but once you have the office approval for your schedule, which you received, then you have to take it home and have it signed by your parents. The final step is to return the schedule to the office. So you've done step one, now you need to do step two: your parents, and then three: bring everything back to school, by next Wednesday. Okay?"

Anna wanted to scream. *No, it's not okay.*

Art was the one thing she was good at, it was the one thing she wanted to do with her life. She wanted to design clothing or buildings, or to paint. It was her dream. She could feel her heart beating hard; it felt as if she were going to explode.

Anna sagged. *My life is over.* They'd make her take typing and she hated typing. Her vision blurred with tears, but she wouldn't cry. She looked down. Her long, dark blonde hair covered her face, hiding her.

Sweeping her hair aside, Anna sat up and began to rub her eyes with the back of her hands to clear her vision. "Okay. Maybe I can talk my parents into the art classes instead of the typing ones they want me to take. I hope..."

Ellen shrugged and Beverly sorted the pile of books in front of her. The warning bell rang and they all stood up.

"Oh, by the way. We won't be able to meet you for lunch anymore," Beverly said as she picked up her books.

"What do you mean?" asked Anna. Her throat got dry and it was hard to swallow.

"She means she is signed up for Chemistry Club, and I've signed up for Library for extra credits." Ellen quickly scooped up her brown lunch bag and tossed it into the garbage bin as they started to walk through the cafeteria doorway.

Anna was confused and hurt. She and Ellen and sometimes Beverly had always talked about things like this. Anna realized that her friends were excluding her and didn't know why.

"Oh, are they taking more people for Library?" asked Anna as she joined her two friends.

"You can try, but I think they were pretty full when I was there this morning." Ellen stopped in the hall beside Anna.

23

"I wish you told me the plan, we could have gone down together and I could have signed up too."

"Yeah, well, I didn't really decide until after I talked to Beverly after homeroom."

"Okay, well, see you later." Anna turned from her friends and walked away down the busy hallway. What else was there to say? This was going to be a very different year for her. *Why should I bother? No friends, crappy classes, no reason to show up at all.*

Anna decided not to meet Ellen after school. They had always walked to school and back home together but today she wasn't in the mood to talk to anyone.

Anna went to her locker; Roger Klassen didn't disappoint her. He hip-checked her, then slammed her locker door into her head, emitting a harsh laugh.

It was the laugh that got to her; the pushing and slamming were one thing, but really, did he have to laugh too? *Enough.* This day had been crappy enough, Roger was going to get both barrels.

She turned and looked him in the eyes.

"Okay, Klassen, or should I say, loser? Why are you always picking on me? This is the second year in a row. Enough with the slamming my locker door into me. Give it a rest, you're not impressing anyone." Anna glanced around at the other students walking down the hall. No one was looking in their direction. "No one cares what you do."

She watched Roger Klassen's red-freckled face go white and his blue eyes started to bulge as he stared at her. Anna shook her head, turned, and retrieved the books she'd need for the next class from her locker, then closed and locked it.

Anna left, shaking her head as she walked away.

It suddenly dawned on her this was the first time she had actually ever spoken to Roger.

Her last class was German. It was usually a little fun, but not today. They had a substitute teacher, so they worked quietly on the next grammar assignment and then had a snap quiz.

"Hi, Anna, how are you?" asked Ingrid, a tall, slender blonde girl sitting next to Anna.

"Fine, Why?"

"You don't look too happy, not like your normal self."

"Yeah, well. Stuff is happening and not all of it's very good."

"Yeah, I know what you mean."

Anna doubted that very much. Ingrid was a really nice, pretty girl, she always had top grades. What could be wrong in her world? Anna bet she got to pick whatever she wanted as an elective.

The final bell rang and Anna took her time to go to her locker and pack her backpack. She checked to make sure she had all her homework and the schedule, then zippered the backpack closed. *I might as well go home so Mom and Dad can make me change the schedule. What does it serve to delay the inevitable?* Nothing.

As she walked down the hall, she stopped by the art class and peeked into the room. Miss Murray stood at the front of the room, cleaning up some of the art supplies. A small woman, with clear gray eyes and short dark hair cut in a pixie style, Miss Murray smiled when she saw Anna in the doorway.

"Anna, just the girl I wanted to see. Can you come here for a minute?"

Anna stepped into the class and walked up to Miss Murray. She was her favorite teacher, so Anna had come to say goodbye. "Miss Murray, I just stopped in to say goodbye. I need my parents to sign off on my schedule and I know my mother will insist I take typing.

I won't be coming to art anymore."

"Oh, Anna, I'm so sorry. I know you really enjoyed this class and you were doing so well." Miss Murray looked at Anna with a concerned expression on her face.

"Would it help if I spoke to your parents? I enjoyed teaching you last year and you are one of my best students. Your fashion sketches and building designs are really very good. I'd love to see you continue."

"I don't know." Anna avoided looking at Miss Murray. Her hands felt damp and she rubbed them on her pants as her mind whirled with possibilities. *Would Miss Murry really do that for me?* Would Miss Murray speaking to her parents maybe change their minds? "Maybe it would work?"

Anna wrote her home phone number on a blank piece of paper, then handed it to Miss Murray. Her heart beat fast and she couldn't stop smiling. *Maybe, just maybe, there is a chance after all.*

***

For Anna, the afternoon and early evening time crawled by. It felt as if she were waiting forever for the phone to ring. She even checked the phone a couple of times to make sure it was working.

Her stomach was in knots and she couldn't eat her dinner. Her mother asked her if she was feeling okay. She just mumbled something. What could she say?

Confused, Anna wondered if should talk to her parents about her courses now, or wait until after Miss Murray called. Anna decided she would give Miss Murray until nine o'clock to call. If she hadn't called by then, Anna would have to show the schedule to her parents and accept whatever they decided.

Anna was sitting on the old green couch in the living room, not paying any attention to the program on the television, when the phone rang. Jumping up, she ran into the kitchen where the house phone was sitting on the counter by the stove. She answered by the second ring. She was breathing hard when she heard Miss Murray's voice. Her mother turned from drying the dishes to look at Anna.

"Mom, Dad, come into the kitchen. The phone is for you," said Anna, trying not to sound too excited, but she could feel her heart race as her hopes soared. Her teacher was actually calling her parents to ask them to have her continue with art class. *I might still have a chance.*

"Yes, they'll be right with you, Miss Murray." Anna handed the phone to her mother as her father entered the kitchen.

Anna couldn't stand the excitement and went into the living room to wait. She could hear their muted conversation from the next room, but her parents weren't saying very much. Then she heard her mother, with her thick German accent, say, "Thank you for calling, but Anna will be taking typing. With typing she can have a job, with painting there is no job. So best for her is typing. Thank you." Anna heard the click of the receiver being placed in the cradle.

Anna's heart sank. She knew her father agreed with her mother.

"Anna. Come here," called her father.

She walked into the kitchen and looked at them. "I'll get my schedule for school." Her eyes were filling with tears blurring her vision, but she came back with her schedule and handed it to her parents. Looking down at the green Arborite kitchen table, her hair fell over her face.

"Come," said her father as he went to sit at the table by the window in the kitchen. She felt her parents' eyes on her as she moved to sit in the chair across from her father.

27

Unable to avoid it any longer, finally Anna looked up at her parents and saw a sad expression in their eyes, but determination too.

"I thought if you heard from my teacher how good I was doing, then I might be able to take art," she whispered.

"What does this mean? It shows you have art here; where is the typing class like we told you?" Her mother handed the form to her father. Anna's mother pressed her lips together as she clenched her jaw.

"Okay, I'm sorry, I changed it. I understand I can get a job with typing, but…I really wanted art."

They wouldn't understand about Roger and the locker, or her friends not including her. Her heart was being squeezed in her chest and her head hurt. She was so alone, so depressed.

Her parents sat looking at her. Anna started to cry softly as her father handed her a pen and she corrected her course selection. He signed it then and patted her hand as he handed it back to her. She knew her parents loved her and wanted the best for her, but now her life was completely empty, with nothing to look forward to.

***

The next morning Anna sat in homeroom when the teacher announced the school was holding a fall art fair in two weeks.

Walking through the halls, Anna heard more and more people talking about what they were doing for the fall fair. After school, Anna popped her head in the art room. She knew it would be polite to thank Miss Murray for calling her parents.

Miss Murray was in and Anna saw Roger at the back of the room. He was drawing something on a large poster.

The heavy cardboard must have been three feet high by two and a half feet wide. It spread over a good portion of an art table.

Watching him, she had to smile; it looked like he was confused. He had a large marker in his hands and kept staring between a small picture in front of him and the large blank poster.

"Hello, Anna. I'm so glad to see you," said Miss Murray as Anna entered the classroom. "You're just the person I wanted to see. I need your help."

Anna shrugged and entered the room. Why did Miss Murray want to see her? *How can I help her? Do what?*

"Anna, I know you're not in art anymore."

"Yes, Miss Murray, I just wanted to say thank you very much for calling yesterday. It really means a lot to me."

"You're very welcome. I'm sorry it didn't turn out the way we hoped. But I do have a project for you if you're willing to accept it," Miss Murray stole a glance at Roger behind her, then continued. "Anna, as you know, we're having an art fair in two weeks. The art department has been asked to do a lot of different things. One of them is to create at least two dozen large posters they want to sell at the fair."

Anna listened carefully as the teacher outlined the art department's involvement in the fair. Her heart sank. It sounded like a lot of fun; unfortunately, she couldn't be involved because she was no longer part of the art department.

"What I've done, because of the short time frame and the huge amount of work, is get permission for extra help from outside the department. So I wonder if you'd be willing to help with the art posters? It's a lot of work. Roger is starting to work on them. Partially to pay off his accumulated detentions and for extra credits.

So you'd be doing him a huge favor if you're willing to work with him. Why don't you think about it and let me know?"

Anna thought she was going to laugh out loud. *Help Roger? Really, why?*

This is the same Roger who had been hurting and embarrassing her. He was the last person she would help.

Anna could see Miss Murray was being serious. Nodding, Anna said, "So you need two dozen posters in two weeks?"

"No, actually we need them in one week, and two dozen is the minimum that I need. The more we make, the more money we make for the art program."

"I see." Anna glanced at Roger and saw he was listening to their conversation with obvious interest.

"Why don't you think about it. And if you know anyone else who might be interested, let me know. I will be able to get you released from some classes for this project."

Roger smiled at her and showed her the small cartoon picture he was using as a template. He had about four pictures he had been given to use; they were all simple, so it shouldn't be hard to do.

After Anna left the art room, she realized not only was Roger polite to her, but he hadn't bothered her at all since she confronted him. Her spirits started to lift as she considered getting involved with this art project.

Anna stood at the entrance to the cafeteria when she heard Ellen's voice behind her.

"There you are. I was looking for you yesterday after school and you didn't come by my locker. I tried calling last night but the phone was busy. Are you all right?" asked Ellen. She appeared concerned, her lips were pursed and her forehead had wrinkles.

"It seems you and Beverly have had a lot to do and none of it involves me."

"And you think we're not friends anymore because we have different interests?"

"Well, kind of, and our interests aren't different. I would have liked to volunteer at the library," said Anna.

"I'm sorry. I should have said something about the library club, but it was a really quick decision I had to make or lose my spot."

Ellen led the way to a table and slid onto the end of the seat. Anna, following her, did the same.

"Tell you what, I just heard a few minutes ago from the librarian that some of the students have already dropped out. Better offers, especially with this fall fair."

"Okay, I'll drop by the library after lunch. When are you volunteering at the library?" asked Anna as she took a bite of her apple. She noticed then that her mother had packed a couple of cookies for her as well, her favorites.

"Only on Wednesday at lunch."

"Okay. I have something to talk to you about after school too. It would be great if you could give me a hand with an art project."

Anna watched as Ellen's eyes widened in surprise. "Your parents let you stay in art? I can't believe it."

"No, they didn't. I'm taking typing. I can see their point of view. I don't agree or like it, but I understand it. Okay, Miss Murray asked me to make a bunch of posters to sell at the fair. We'll need help."

"That sounds like fun," said Ellen.

"It will be fun." Anna outlined her ideas to Ellen. The more Anna talked, the more excited she was getting.

"What about your art class?" asked Ellen.

"I realized today there will be lots of opportunities for me to paint and do art. My taking art classes may be delayed a little, maybe even a lot, but it's not the end of my dream," said Anna and she felt much better about her art and future.

Honeymoon

This frightening tale answers the question do we really know anyone even those we love?

THE NEW MRS. JAKE BROCK, as of six hours ago, glared at their honeymoon cottage in Cold Lake, British Columbia, from the passenger seat of their four-wheel-drive silver Toyota. Then she scanned the brochure in her hands to compare the picture with the reality in front of her. This was nothing like the brochure, or what they had been told it would be. *What a horrible dump.*

Melanie Brock, a petite woman in her midtwenties with blue eyes, a golden suntan, and a slim figure, loved to laugh. Many people were naturally drawn to her sense of humor and easy manner.

Except when you crossed her. *Never* cross her.

She could feel the blood pounding in her ears as she got angrier and angrier. *How could they have lied to us?*

Melanie tucked her shoulder-length, dark blonde hair behind her ears and moved her sunglasses to the top of her head. She struggled to calm herself by not thinking about the situation as she opened her purse to check her makeup. She usually wore only a little eyeliner, mascara, and lip gloss, but this was a special occasion; she wanted to look her very best for Jake.

After retrieving her mirror from her blue leather hobo purse, she applied a little more lip gloss and fluffed up her bangs.

Perfect, now I look better, she thought, taking a deep breath and studying herself in the mirror.

The cabin was located in a small valley ringed by the foothills of the Rocky Mountains. The forest around them was dense with firs, cedars, pines, and ferns. Around the brilliant blue lake next to the cabin stood tall maple and birch trees; the air should have been fresh and invigorating, yet it reeked of skunk.

She looked at the moss-covered, sway-backed cabin roof, the screen door hanging to one side, the missing boards on the porch, and a bashed-in aluminum garbage can. *I was wrong. A dump looks better than this derelict.*

"Look, babe, isn't it great?" asked Jake, her new husband, a tall, athletic man in his late twenties with dark brown hair and emerald-green eyes. He jumped out of the driver's side of the Toyota.

Theirs had been a whirlwind romance and wedding after only knowing each other for two weeks.

Melanie got out of the passenger side and headed to the back of the car to start unpacking.

"Good idea; you unpack the car. I'm going to take a quick look at the lake first, then lie down for a nap. That was a tough drive. Let me know when you've got dinner ready," he said as he headed to the old rickety dock sticking out into the lake.

"Jake, I hadn't planned on making dinner tonight. I'm pretty bushed with the wedding this afternoon and everything. I thought we were going out to have a bite in town?"

"Babe, I just drove for four hours and the last hour was a twisting, rough gravel road. I'm not driving back to town tonight. You realize Cold Lake is a town in name only, don't you? It's three streets by three streets, without a single stoplight.

It has one bar, two coffee shops, one gas station combined with a general store, and an old fashioned diner. Exactly where are you planning to go for a fancy dinner?"

Jake's tone was mocking as he walked past the loaded truck to the lake.

He could have at least picked up his own suitcase from the back of the car and carried it inside before he went to the lake.

Melanie studied the tall dark fir and pine trees that seemed to surround the little cabin on all sides, cutting off any light or air. She turned to look at the lake and saw Jake standing looking out at the green, quiet, still water.

The sandy beach was actually moss-covered rocks amongst tall grass and weeds. There was a rough wooden rowboat up on the beach, but it looked old, grey, and heavy. She wondered if it would even float.

Jake passed her and smiled as he opened the hanging screen door and the blue wooden door, passing the car without lifting a finger to help her.

Melanie stared at Jake's back; he hadn't even bothered to help. He even left his suitcase for her to take care of. He was just like Conrad. She started to hum a tuneless song under her breath that sounded like a hive of bees getting ready to swarm. She forced herself to smile and started carrying the heavy suitcases, then the groceries, into the cabin.

After she dropped their groceries in the main room, she took a quick look around.

There was a sofa and a chair on one side of the main room with a coffee table in the center. In the far corner was a wood stove, and along the wall was a counter with a faucet and basin. There was an upper cabinet that contained plates and glasses.

There was a small table under the window by the door with two chairs facing the window. There was a short hallway, and it seemed there was a doorway on the left, probably the bedroom, and a back door straight back.

She could hear Jake already softly snoring from the bedroom. She looked in the room; all it contained was a queen bed with a sagging mattress, covered by the faded brown quilt that he was stretched out on, and a battered nightstand. She quietly stacked their suitcases in an alcove in the bedroom. At least they would be out of the way.

Next she methodically put away the food they'd brought with them in the kitchen. They had only brought some basic supplies so it didn't take long to unpack and soon everything was put away. She hadn't really planned on doing any cooking; after all, this was her honeymoon and Jake had told her he would take care of everything.

Until now, she hadn't realized there wasn't a television, computer, or telephone. She checked her cell phone. It didn't work here, no bars at all. She managed to find a checker set, a cribbage board, and a deck of mushy paper playing cards.

They wanted time alone without any distractions for their honeymoon, a chance to really get to know each other. It seemed that these amenities, or lack of, certainly fulfilled their shared desire of no distractions.

She checked for the barbeque the brochure mentioned, hoping they could grill steaks for dinner. Unfortunately, it was a mass of rust and grease, so that plan was out.

Maybe she'd feel better after a nice long soak. But not in this cabin—the toilet was an outhouse thirty feet away, behind the back door, along a muddy path amongst the trees. The outside of the back door was painted a bright, glossy red.

I wonder if it glows in the dark so you can see your way home?

Looking up, Melanie realized while it was only afternoon in July, heavy clouds were rolling in. It would be getting dark soon and in these tall rugged mountains, probably cold too.

She didn't want to eat too early so she made sure they had sufficient wood to build a fire in the wood stove later on. She went back to the wood box and brought in the rest of the wood, she hoped they would have enough for the night. Tomorrow, if they were still here, they would have to chop more. She's seen some dry rounds under a tarp at the back of the cabin. She didn't know how to chop wood and hoped Jake did if not she would be learning something new on this trip.

Melanie found a flashlight on the bedroom nightstand next to her snoring husband. In the main room, there was an oil lamp on the table and the small wood stove. She was leery, but the stove appeared to be the only thing they'd be able to cook on. It might hold two frying pans and a small pot for hot water to make coffee or just for hot water. Perhaps they could light a fire outside in the fire pit she saw near where they parked the car.

She felt her energy start to drop; she knew she was tired. It was time for a large glass of water and a short nap. She joined Jake on the bed, lying down on top of the quilt. She fell asleep within seconds of her head hitting the pillow.

***

Melanie woke when she felt Jake move next to her and his warm body leave the bed. She stretched her arms over her head and realized how quiet it was and how dark. She couldn't see her hand in front of her face, or anything else.

She was scared, she'd never been in such absolute darkness before in her life.

"Jake, are you there? I can't see anything," she called out to her husband. She heard her heart thud loudly in her ears as she strained to listen for any other noises.

She heard a thud, followed by Jake swearing. She rolled over and picked up the flashlight from the nightstand. She shone it to find Jake sitting on the floor holding his foot.

"Are you hurt?"

"No, just stubbed my toe. I'll be fine." Jake got up from the floor.

"I'll put on the oil lamp. I think there's a generator at the back of the cabin. I saw matches by the stove too," said Melanie.

Soon the lamp was lit. The glass chimney was dirty, so the light was weak.

"I'll check on the generator after dinner, is it ready?" Jake walked to the table and sat down.

Melanie looked at Jake, sitting at the table, as she walked into the main room. Just like Daddy.

"Not yet, it will only take a few minutes. But I need to get the wood stove going first." Melanie looked at the stove, trying to figure out how it worked.

"You have the lamp, how about giving me the flashlight and I'll check the generator while you make dinner?" asked Jake as he held out his hand.

She opened the stove and saw that a fire had been laid for them. *Good stuff, maybe this place won't be too bad after all*. Relived, she struck a match and in no time had the stove warming up. It did a nice job of heating up the cabin. She found salt and pepper shakers in the cupboards with plates. Soon she was frying the steaks while she made the salad and rinsed the shrimp.

She was hungry and the food smelled really good. Her stomach started growling; she could definitely eat.

"I'm starving. Sure smells good and looks cozy in here," said Jake when he returned to the kitchen from outside. "No luck with the generator, it won't start." He put his arms around Melanie and kissed her neck as he held her tight against him.

She returned the embrace, then moved back to flip the sizzling steaks. "I thought I heard thunder, Jake. Is it starting to rain?"

"Yeah, and it's getting cold, too. But we'll be fine in here. We'll have dinner and then … oh, there's no television?" he said, looking around the room at the meager furniture and amenities.

"You're right, babe, no television or internet, no phone, and no cell reception. But we do have a couch with matching chair, a table with two chairs, and a couple of games and a worn deck of cards. I'm sure that we can keep ourselves entertained." She thought of the pretty little nighty she had packed for tonight; she hoped he would like it.

"I don't play games."

"Well, I know you don't like to gamble, sweetie, but card games are different."

"No. I don't ever play games." His eyes narrowed as he glared at her.

"No problem. I have my e-reader, a spare book, and a crossword puzzle book."

Jake scowled as he looked around the cabin.

"Look, there are books for you, too," Melanie said. "Some about ghosts and some about the early settlers in this area. Maybe you can try one of them?"

"Yeah, you're right. Is dinner ready?"

39

Honeymoon

Melanie smiled to herself as she nodded at her new husband. As her dear mother so often says, a way to a man's heart is through his stomach.

***

Jake had cleaned up after dinner while Melanie was sitting on the couch reading and enjoying a cup of hot tea, all of her favorite things to do. Jake had gone outside a while ago to try the generator again. He hadn't returned for a long time and she was growing concerned about him.

Jake seemed like an active person, not one to sit still for very long. There may not be enough for him to do in this little cabin in the woods.

The back door banged against the wall as Jake walked back in. He struggled to close it against the strong wind blowing in from outside. Through the open door, she heard the sound of heavy rain pelting down hard against the wooden porch. It seemed the storm had settled directly overhead. "Still no luck with the generator," he said after finally managing to get the door closed.

"Oh? I found some old maps you might be interested in."

Jake brushed the rain from his clothes and slicked back his hair with the palms of both hands. He nodded to her. "That sounds interesting. Maybe I can figure out some hiking trails we could try if this weather ever breaks."

He came over to sit beside her, then leaned toward her and kissed her full on the lips. Her insides were warmed by his touch. Her new husband was an incredible kisser.

There was a sudden gust of wind that shook the roof and rattled the windows, then everything went completely quiet.

In a few minutes, the storm was back; the wind seemed even stronger than before.

"Come on, I'll show you how to play Honeymoon Bridge," she said brightly. "It's really easy and fun. We'll keep score, but not bet. How's that?"

Jake looked at her, his eyes narrowed as his lips pressed together in a thin line. "Okay, we'll try it," he said at last. "But if either one of us doesn't like it, we stop. Agreed?"

Melanie held up the battered deck of cards she'd found earlier. "Absolutely. There are lots of different rules and variations, but this is what we played as kids.

"The deck is fifty-two cards, I've counted them and they're all here. We deal out thirteen cards to each player, the rest are extra so we don't use them. We have five rounds per game. It's based on bridge. Each game ends after we've played five rounds. The trump cards go by suit: clubs, diamonds, hearts, spades, and lastly no trump. You have to follow suit. If you don't have any of that suit, then you have to play another card from any other suit. It can be a trump or another card.

"At the end we will have thirteen tricks; the one with the most tricks wins. We can play a practice hand first if you like. How does that sound?"

"Sure, let's practice," Jake said, seeming enthused.

Melanie quickly shuffled and dealt thirteen cards to each of them. Jake got the hang of Honeymoon Bridge quickly in the practice round, so Melanie found a half sheet of paper and lined it with four columns. The first column showed who dealt. In the second she would record the trump suit for each round; in the third and fourth she would record the score for each player for each round. At the top of the third and fourth columns, she wrote their names.

41

"Oh, we also keep track of how many tricks we have. If you win more than seven tricks, you've won that round. The person who wins three or more rounds wins the game. Any questions?" she asked.

Jake shook his head "no."

"Fine, how long do you want to play?"

"I don't know what you're asking," said Jake.

"We keep track of how many games we've played. Over an evening, we might play fifty games; during a weekend maybe one hundred, or even five hundred. How many games would like to start with tonight?"

Jake nodded that he understood. "Let's try for one hundred. But if we want to end earlier, we can always continue later, right?" His eyebrows arched as he grinned at her.

They started to play and Jake soon began to relax. It seemed he was having fun.

They had ten quick games and it was almost even. Melanie was ahead by only five points.

She watched Jake play. Gradually his manner started to change and he became very serious. His eyes darted back and forth. The tip of his tongue stuck out from between his lips. He leaned forward, watching every move intently, his eyes focused, never leaving the cards.

Jake reminded her of a cat watching a mouse, ready to pounce.

She didn't like his intensity. It reminded her of people she had known in her life that were poor sports and really bad winners and worse losers.

She could feel her temper start to rise and she couldn't let that happen. This was her honeymoon. She quickly calmed herself.

"All righty, I think it may be time to go to the little outhouse and then get ready for bed, my little wife. Do you want to go first?" Jake took Melanie's hand and smoothed his thumb over her fingers.

"That would be great." Melanie got up and left by the back door.

She came back a few minutes later and there was Jake, shuffling the cards. "How about one more quick game?" he said as he started to deal.

What is he doing? This is our wedding night.

She shivered in her thin nightgown and shawl, then sat down watching her husband deal. "Sure. I'm glad you're enjoying this game. Is it cold in here?"

She walked to the stove and opened it. Tendrils of pungent wood smoke and ash drifted out the door into the cabin. Looking inside, she picked up the poker and started to poke at the glowing embers.

"Melanie, are you coming or are you going to stand there all night?"

"Actually, we may have a problem. The fire is out. I'm going to try to light it again. We only have a little kindling left, so wish me luck."

Melanie very carefully took the few scraps of kindling and put it into the still warm stove. "Actually, you know what? I'm going outside to see if I can find some dry pinecones or grass so we have tinder for our fire. I'll be back in a few minutes. I think I know where I can find some easily."

Melanie pulled on two sweatshirts, two pair of socks, and her running shoes. Just as she opened the back door, there was a crash by the front door.

Oh my God, what was that? Melanie's heart pounded hard as she slammed the door closed and locked it. She was terrified.

"Jake, what was that?" whispered Melanie as she silently tiptoed to stand next to Jake.

"Shush, listen," Jake whispered.

They both crouched by the front door and listened. Through the door came soft woofing and snorting sounds, then the garbage can bounced around, followed by a heavy thump. Something large was moving around on the porch.

Jake motioned to Melanie to walk with him to the back of the room.

"Babe, what did you do with the packages of the meat scraps, shrimp peels, and the beef bones?" he whispered, his warm breath caressing her cheek.

Melanie suddenly realized what he was getting to. "I just threw the garbage from dinner into the garbage cans. Oh, dear, it's a bear, isn't it?"

"Yeah, it sounds too big to be a raccoon."

"We've got to get wood for the fire or we'll freeze to death." Melanie's voice started getting higher and louder. Her whole body was shaking and she couldn't stop trembling.

He chuckled softly. "No. That's not going to happen. We'll put on the lamp and wait until he leaves. We can play cards while we wait. I'm sure once the bear realizes there is nothing else in there, he'll leave."

"It would really help if we could get that generator going; then, at least, we'd have heat and light. Jake, I'm really afraid." Her voice shook. She hated the fear in her voice, but she hated how scared she was even more.

They played cards for an hour. Everything had been quiet for a long time.

"What do you think?" she asked after recording the last round's scores. Since the first game they played, Jake had only won two other times and it seemed that he was getting moody.

Melanie arched her back. Her back was really starting to hurt after sitting on the hard chairs for the last hour. "I need to change positions. I'm going to read for a while, okay? I think if we give it another hour, the bear'll be gone."

"I'd really rather play cards," Jake said in a whiney tone. "I feel like my luck is going to change. I'm in for a lucky streak very soon. Come on, give me a chance to win and catch up."

Melanie gaped at her husband; she didn't like the look in his eyes. It had a gleam and the way he was dealing seemed urgent as if he were under some strange power. He was slamming down the cards and his mouth was a thin line. She could see beads of sweat forming on his brow. Odd. It wasn't like it was hot in the cabin.

"Okay, babe, just calm down. It's only a kid's game," Melanie said as she rolled her shoulders and arched her back.

"Quit telling me what to do," he growled. "Sure, it's easy to be condescending when you're ahead. What are you doing, gloating now? Let's play a few more games." He grabbed the cards and began shuffling. "Okay, this time I'll keep score. We'll see how the game goes when I keep score. Do we have any more paper? This little bit is almost full." He seemed frantic. Obsessed.

Melanie was growing angry and a little scared; her heart pounded hard and her palms were damp with perspiration. She didn't like having a bear hanging around outside, that was one thing. But her husband going crazy inside a cabin in the middle of nowhere was something even scarier. There was no one to call for help. If Jake went crazy, she'd have to deal with him herself.

She watched him deal the cards. His left eye twitched as he stared wild-eyed at his cards, then he smirked. She didn't know what to do. Her hands were wet and she dried them on her sweats. She noticed that her hands were shaking, too.

This was supposed to be their honeymoon. This was supposed to be a romantic, magical time. In her dreams of their first days of married life, she had envisioned wining, dining, going for long walks on the beach, talking and laughing as they learned more about each other. *I should never have suggested this stupid game.*

She sat in silence. Maybe she should throw a game or two to see if Jake calmed down. She looked at her cards. It was no trump and she had two aces, three kings, and a queen, with seven cards in her strongest suit. She felt her heart sink. There was no way she could do much with this hand except win.

She pulled back her hair and tied it. She felt herself start to gnaw on her bottom lip, a childhood habit that she had worked hard on breaking. She saw Jake watching her, smiling.

"So you do have tells, do you? Good to know, good to know," he said to himself and nodded.

Melanie took a deep breath. *What is he talking about?* Did he think by playing a kid's game, he was now some hot shot gambler?

That game she won ten tricks. She was lucky to slough off the three she had given him.

"Okay, babe, it's your turn to deal." Jake said. "Remember, I'll be watching you. If you let me win, I'll be checking your cards. We'll have no cheating. I'll win, but I'll win fair and square."

The wind outside the walls howled, the roof shook, and the windows rattled around them. Melanie shivered as she looked at the deck of cards. Her hands were turning blue.

She rubbed and blew on them, hoping to warm them before she started dealing the next hand.

"Be careful there, girl," Jake warned, his voice an unpleasant growl. "Don't try dealing from the bottom of the deck. I'm watching you."

She gave him a weak smile and swallowed hard. Thank goodness they didn't have any booze with them, she couldn't image what he would be like if he were drunk. Then she remembered she had brought a bottle of very nice wine, but he didn't know about it. It would keep for another day.

An angry, terrible roar came from the outside, and the walls shook. This was followed by a growl and a deep, huffing noise. They looked at each other, the game forgotten.

One corner of the cabin was hit by a heavy weight again. Something was pounding on the walls. Then they heard something the size of a truck land on their front deck, shaking the windows as it passed.

They heard a high keening, followed by a ripping sound tearing into the cabin's wooden walls. Then came such an awful stench their eyes watered and breathing became hard.

"Skunk," Melanie said as she tried to cover her nose and mouth with her hands.

It was as if they opened their mouths and a foul smelling, vinegary substance was being poured down their throats. Melanie wanted to throw open the door and run, but she knew they were trapped.

She wanted to roll into a ball in the corner of the room and scream. Her stomach heaved and she tasted bile at the back of her throat. She was going to throw up. She knew that neither action would help.

After taking a deep breath, then slowly exhaling, her mind hit a wall and she started calming down. She closed her eyes. *Oh, thank you.* She hadn't gone into a blind rage like before.

It took a long time before the smell started to go away and they could talk.

Jake looked at Melanie through watering eyes. "That's a bear?"

Melanie smiled at him. "Yeah, and it sounds like it just tangled with a skunk. I'm not sure who won, but it wasn't us." She looked at him, dropping her cards onto the table. She rubbed her hands together.

"Babe, can I talk to you about something?" she asked gently once she got her breath back. Jake nodded, but before she could say any more, they heard the bear suddenly begin to bat the garbage cans around, huffing all the while. Melanie's words stuck in the back of her throat.

After a while they heard the bear leave the porch, its heavy, ambling footsteps moving away into the brush surrounding the cabin. The bear was finally leaving.

"I just realized there's no way we can even wash anything or have a shower," Jake said as he leaned back and put his cards on the table.

They waited. Silence.

"You were saying?" he asked, reaching for her hand.

She looked down at their joined hands, her cold one in his warm one. She knew she would have to choose her words carefully. She let out a slow breath, then looked at him.

"Um, I have an idea," he said, his gaze dropping to look down at their joined hands.

"I think that we should use this score sheet and the cards as kindling to light the fire. Do you think that would work?" he asked.

She leaned over, picked up the paper and cards, folded the score sheet in half and twisted it, and handed it to him.

"Mr. Jake Brock, that sounds like a fine idea indeed. Let me give it a go. I'll see how much of the dried wood we have inside I can break and shave off. I think, if I'm careful, we should have a good base to start a fire."

"I'll try and break the wood into smaller chunks too." Jake paused, then continued. "Babe, I'm not going to play cards anymore. I don't like the way it makes me feel and act." He let out a deep sigh.

Melanie took the paper and cards and added them to their pile of kindling; Jake added his shaved wood. She carefully put their collection into the stove and lit it.

"That sounds like a plan to me," Melanie said, her heart beating rapidly with excitement.

This was the man she loved and the man she married. "Besides, we don't need to play Honeymoon Bridge, there are lots of other things to do."

She looked at him and smiled. She felt the knot in her stomach ease as the fire caught and started warming the cabin.

She realized she was happy. Tonight she hadn't gotten angry or had to kill another husband, and that was a very good thing.

Graybill

A tale of a dragon king and a deadly quest.

MY LEGS WERE screaming and my back was starting to go into spasms. But I knew if I moved I'd face death. I had to hold this curtsey or die trying.

The room smelled like the impersonal cold hard marble floor I was standing on. Even though I could hear a fire crackling and sputter in the smallest Audience Chamber in the castle, it was icy cold.

The very worst would be if I fell over and Gwen didn't. There was no way my sister would win this competition. She's a wonderful sister. She has deep blue eyes like mine, but has thick, dark red hair that she wears loose; she's slender and at five foot eight inches tall for a woman, has healing power and loved her plants. You noticed Gwen when she entered a room.

I have long blonde hair that I braid every morning to keep out of my face, with a small nose over full lips but only five foot four. My figure is a little on the full side. I paint, love to sing and see auras.

"Your majesty, Artist Sofia Jaffrey is here as you requested." The court Jester, Jason called to me. I heard the bells on his costume jingling.

I dug my thumbnail into my index finger to keep myself from laughing.

50

I often wonder what he looks like.

Jason, my beloved, wouldn't show me his Jester's uniform. Was it a red costume with gold bells? Or blue with silver? Did he juggle and do tumbling? He played the guitar and had a lovely voice. I know he trained hard for a solid six months before he took over from the previous Jester.

I waited. I knew I couldn't move unless given permission to do so.

I heard a rustle of clothing a few feet from me, but I didn't look to see who it was. I was a decent painter but an excellent forger, also someone who could see the auras surrounding people and sense their moods. It all came in handy when you were negotiating a hard bargain and had to sell people something they didn't want or need.

I felt myself start to wobble as I started to lose my balance. I focused on my breathing and managed to regain my balance again. I heard my sister breathing next to me. Her breaths were coming out in little puffs of cloud.

Gwen was an incredibly talented healer and herbalist. She could grow anything.

Which worked out well in our family. I would almost kill a plant and she would heal it, then I would paint it.

"Also, Healer Gwen Jaffrey, as you requested," announced the Jester. Again I heard the bells and wondered what the Jester was doing. What I didn't hear was the King laughing.

I looked at the white marble floor and followed a green vein until it was out of my sight. Steady. I am a steady rock. I am a wobbling rock. NO...

"Please rise," said the King of Graybill. I heard the swishing sounds of heavy robes and the dragging sound made by the King's tail.

I couldn't move, my right foot was asleep, and my left knee had locked. I couldn't get up, but I had to. The King commanded it.

In that instant I heard the bells from the Jester again and realized someone had landed close by me. I tipped my head up now saw Jason, the new court Jester, in a low bow. His hand was stretched out for me to take in mine. I did and recovered from my almost fall.

He was wearing a dark gray and white costume, complete with tri-cornered hat trimmed in red with gold bells. It suited him, set off his dark gold eyes and dark curly shoulder length hair. He was clean-shaven. His face had gotten more angular and his chin firmer over the last year. It dawned on me my childhood sweetheart had grown into a man.

As I stood I noticed he held out a hand for Gwen as well. That made me feel better, I wasn't the only person who almost embarrassed herself.

We stood in front of our magnificent Dragon King dressed in a deep golden floor-length vest made of thick satin trimmed at the hem and sleeves with snow-white ermine.

The King stood straight and tall on a raised dais in front of the Throne Room next to the royal thrones surveying those below him.

The king was truly a gorgeous creature. He was about ten feet tall, broad through the shoulders with a massive thirty-foot wingspan. Currently his belly was a deep crimson color, which indicated he was preparing to mate.

His magnificent head and back were covered with thick royal purple scales and his eyes glowed the deep amber the color of honey. His body was long and sinewy with six legs ending in a long, tapered tail.

The Jester, Jason, stepped back and the three of us stood side by side looking up at the King waiting for him to speak. I noticed there were at least twenty other people in the room. Clerks, scribes, advisors, and court followers were all milling around waiting for the pleasure of the King.

The throne room's ceiling was twenty feet high, with a white marble floor, and a wall of ceiling to floor windows. There were two thrones on a dais at the front of the room where the King and Queen sat. A massive stone fireplace ran from the floor to the beamed ceiling opposite the wall of windows. It looked large enough to cook three full-grown oxen easily. Of the three throne rooms I knew this was the smallest, a more intimate room.

I looked at, Gwen, my twin. We were fraternal twins so almost completely opposite in coloring, aptitude, and attitude. We gave our parents a tough time growing up. Not intentionally, but our taste in most things were opposite. Whatever Gwen liked I didn't. Our parents had a real handful with us, but they loved us and we loved them. So it worked out.

It seemed the only thing Gwen and I had in common, besides our love of family, was our very strong intuition.

"I want everyone to leave the room, except my Jester and the Ladies."

"But, Sire?" said Sir Tomas, one of the King's senior advisors.

"Now!" The word had a deep roar behind it as the King turned to look at Sir Tomas. The King's eyes grew a deep gold color slowly starting to swirl like a hypnotic disk.

Sir Tomas's dark complexion paled as he bowed and hurried from the room.

A deep sigh came from between the King's taught lips as the room finally cleared of everyone but the King, Jason, and us.

"Ladies, I need your help," said the King when we were alone.

We waited for him to continue. I looked at him, his eyes had calmed and stopped swirling. I saw his aura was yellow and green, tinged with red. The yellow was energy, green health, but the red anger or worry. Not very good in a dragon, it indicated a heavy heart and deep worry.

I hadn't looked at Gwen yet I knew she would be watching and reading him as well. If needed she would send him healing power to strengthen him as well. We'd compare notes later.

"How can we serve?" Gwen and I said in unison as we bowed from the waist.

"Come closer," he said in his throaty growl.

We moved forward toward the King until we stood close to the largest throne in the room. His majesty arranged his tail and robe then sat.

Jason was at our side. When he stopped we did.

"This conversation will not leave this room. Our Queen has need of you ladies. She is waiting in the Royal chambers. Jester, go with the ladies and deliver them to the Queen."

Gwen and I had agreed, when we received the summons to the castle, that no matter what happened, we would turn down their request. We had enough to do with keeping ourselves alive without going on some silly quest.

Our long formal stiff gowns trailing after us as we walked across the marble floor to the corner of the room where there was a set of tall oak doors I hadn't noticed before. Jason opened one of them then led us out of the throne room.

**

We walked into the Queens chamber together.

This was a smaller room than the Throne Room we were in. But still the bedroom was very large, and ornate enough for a Dragon Queen.

There was a large mahogany desk, with a massive high backed upholstered armchair behind it set against one wall. Another wall had red and orange drapes and opposite that was a large fireplace. A blazing fire illuminated the room. The fire was hot; it felt as if there was no air in the room, I was suffocating. I thought I might pass out. My face felt feverish and my heart rate had accelerated. I tried to swallow but my tongue stuck to the roof of my mouth.

I waved my hand in front of my face as I looked for a place to sit, but there was nowhere. There had to be a window I could open. Quickly I strode over to the window and threw back the draperies. I discovered a lovely tall window looking out over the expansive sun kissed gardens.

I grabbed the window latch, turned it, and pushed the window open. A rush of fresh air washed over me and I leaned close to the opening, gulping in oxygen as quickly as I could.

"Oh, Lord, what have you done?" asked Jason his eyes large as his face went pale.

"Exactly what she should have," answered Gwen as she moved to my side and put the curtains back to where they had hung to cover up most of the air coming into the room.

I could still feel the flow of cool air coming from the window. The air would cool the room, but no very slowly.

"My Queen," Gwen said as she curtsied.

My heart sank and my knees protested at the very idea of a curtsey.

"Oh, no. Please don't do that. I asked you to come here and I thank you for coming so quickly," said the Queen.

Moving from the shadows in one corner of the room appeared my Queen. She was shorter than the King and stood seven feet tall, a good height for a female dragon. She wore a gown of yellow and lavender, which was open in the front. I saw her belly, rather than being a mating bright scarlet red, was a sickly greenish orange. Something was definitely wrong. As I looked at her aura, I saw a whirling of yellow and blue with a thick outline of eggplant purple rimmed with red. Not good at all.

I looked at Gwen and she nodded to me. She was sending the Queen healing energy, now we had to determine where her problem lay.

Gwen was an expert with human healing but I didn't know how much information she had on helping dragons.

"My Queen, may I and my sister, the healer, confer for a moment?"

"Oh, please, but please hurry. You have to do something. I need help. But I can't do it ... I just can't. It's too terrifying." The Queen wrung her hands together her long black talons clicking together as tears flowing down her cheeks.

I backed up slowly hoping Gwen would follow my lead. She did and met me by the door.

"The Queen's an absolute mess. Isn't she and the King were supposed to go to the Royal nesting spot in the Forest of Graybill's King?" I asked as I looked over at the Queen. I smiled and nodded to Gwen as if we were agreeing on something. The Queen stopped crying, looking at us hopefully.

"Yes, they are to leave in two weeks. We need to find out what the problem is. Then decide on a course of action," Gwen said.

"Okay, we need to ask her direct questions to come up with a treatment plan. Should we ask Jason to leave? Or let the Queen decide?" As I spoke I realized my hands were damp from the heat and the stress of being here. I wanted to wipe them on my dress but knew I couldn't. The dress was my mother's and she made me promise to bring it back the way I found it, in perfect condition.

We walked back to join the Queen. She had taken the seat behind the desk, her color and aura looked better now.

"Ladies, I asked you here because of Gwen's healing arts, and Sofia, your painting and skill as a forger. But most importantly you both have inquiring, logical minds. That's what I need right now.

"Jason, please bring me a glass of cold water from the kitchen." The Queen nodded at Jason, he turned to the door and hurried off, the ringing of his bells soon faded into the distance.

My heart swelled with pride. He was a good man. Jason and I were hand fasted, but no one knew that except our immediate families.

Gwen and I turned toward the Queen. She motioned us closer and we moved ahead until we almost touched her knee. She leaned down, looked around the room then told us what the problem was.

"Ladies, I am terrified. I need you to investigate a haunting in the Forest of Graybill's King." She looked at us, measuring our response.

"The forest is well known to us," I explained. "We live on the outskirts of the forest and so does Jason's family. We've never heard of any haunting."

"I know, that's why I asked you to come. I heard it on good authority that there is a ghost in the forest. It's been seen near the nesting grounds in the last six months. I am terrified. I cannot, will not, go to the nesting area if it is haunted."

Her eyes narrowed. "Therefore there will be no breeding this year. Which means there will be no heir to the throne of Graybill. If *we* do not breed this year, the King's crown will be open to challengers. I and Graybill will go to the winner."

My mouth started to open, before my brain charged in and closed it. I looked at Gwen.

The country of Graybill has had the same unbroken line of Dragon Royalty for five hundred years. We have had peace and our lands have prospered all these centuries.

The Queen continued, "This is mid February, you have until the end of this month to find and destroy this ghost, and bring me proof it is gone. Only then will the King and I perform our duty. I need you to save our kingdom. "

We heard Jason come back. He was carrying a large goblet, the size of his head, in both of his hands. He leaned forward and held the goblet stretched out in front of him offering it to the Queen. "My Queen," he said, bowing his head as he stepped forward.

She looked at him took the cup, drank and continued.

"You may tell Jason what I have told you. He will go with you. Jason, you are to report back to me within one week and let me know of your progress. Do you understand?" The Queen's dark emerald eyes were steady, her regal bearing was back with a certain determination.

As we left, I realized we were being sent out to investigate we were never asked or given a choice.

***

Gwen, Jason, and I entered Upper Umber on horseback, the town we grew up in. It was a cool morning but the sun was trying to shine through the grey clouds. We were pleased to see the town remained much as we left it. There were two towns on the Blue River and Lower Umber. Upper Umber was across from Lower. The town was high in the mountains surrounded by thick forests of pines and massive oaks and meadows. From the alpine meadows you had a wonderful view of the entire valley and river far below.

The town was also close to the Royal Nest, an aerie, in a tall rocky mound of steep stone and cliffs the sacred birthing place of the dragons called The Forest of Graybill's King. It had been the place where future Kings were conceived, and where they were born, since the beginning of time.

Gwen and I explained to Jason what the Queen had told us of our quest and stressed that we were not to share this information with anyone else.

We dropped off the horses at the town stable and took our packs of clothing and sundries with us. The sun had come out and a gentle breeze with it.

The town was perched on a cliff jutting from the side of the mountain. The towns houses were narrow, some two floors, but most with three. Most of the older homes were Tudor style houses with heavy beams, sprinkled among them were a few newer chalets.

It was wonderful walking along the hard, dirt road of Upper Umber in the fresh clean air, and warm sunshine, being greeted by my friends and family. Since the apparition in the forest had been seen by several of the people who lived in town it would be a good idea to check out their stories.

"Let's plan this visit," I suggested to my sister and Jason. "I think it would be best if we went to Jason's home first to visit his younger brother and mother. Jason have you been home since your Dad's funeral last month?" I spoke gently knowing this was a difficult topic for him.

"No. Mum, wrote me once since the funeral, but I couldn't reply. I didn't know what to say."

"Okay, let's check in on her first, see how's she's doing. We'll see how your brother, Ethan, is as well. He's thirteen now isn't he?"

"Yes, A difficult age to lose a father. Has anyone heard anything about the accident?" asked Gwen.

"No, just that father was found at the bottom of the cliffs of the Nesting site. It appeared a rock slide crushed him," Jason said, his tone suggested he was skeptical of this finding.

"Your home hasn't changed very much has it?" I asked as we started walking up the steep streets. "What if after our visit we see Mum and Dad too," I said to Gwen. "Then go to the Jay and Otter for lunch?"

We would have to limit our time visiting our parents. I looked at Gwen. She sighed obviously having the same thought. We didn't get holidays often and hadn't seen our parents in a while.

In the castle area we shared a small house in a good location and we supported ourselves, she with her healing arts, and me with my paintings.

Lately it seemed there was an influx of healers into the kingdom. In most towns there seemed to be a sign offering the services of a new healer appearing almost every day. And while I had new ideas for subjects I'd like to try painting, I stayed with the saleable subjects customers liked. Maybe one day I'd gather the courage to be different.

"All we can do is to let them know we are on business and are only stopping by for a short visit. I expect they will demand we stay longer, but if we promise to be back before the end of fall, perhaps that will appease them. What do you think?"

"I hate to say it but your right, Sofia. But I'm going to need the two of you to help me leave. My heart feels so heavy I should have returned before now. What kind of son am I?" Jason's eyes started to fill with tears.

I watched him. We'd had this conversation and I knew I couldn't ease his pain, only time would.

"You're a good son, Jason. And your mother knows it. You're also a good brother to thirteen-year-old Ethan. You may want to send them the odd letter occasionally. Can you send them any money?" Gwen asked gently as we turned up the street to where Jason used to live.

Jason hung his head. "No, I can't right now. My new job as a Juggler doesn't pay well, but there are openings for a gardener and a stable hand coming up soon. Those positions pay more."

I could see him as a gardener, he loved plants, he had a natural touch with growing things.

"Let's get on with it then," Gwen said brightly as we walked up to the front door of the two-story cabin. We stood to one side and let Jason knock. We waited. I looked around the yard. It seemed to be well maintained. It was still cold and the bushes and plants were bare, but the yard was neat and tidy.

"Oh, my, Jason," said a very happy mother after she opened the door. I watched Jason being hugged and kissed soundly on both cheeks. He was blushing, but allowing his mother to show her affection. He hugged and held her too. After they finished, they both had tears in their eyes but smiles on their faces.

61

"Oh, you brought guests," said his mother when she spotted Gwen and I standing on the stoop beside the door. "Please come in, Sofia, Gwen. I'm just ready to put on the kettle. Please join me."

Hi mother stepped back to open the door wider and loudly called out into the neighborhood, "Ethan, please come home. Your brother and his friends have come to visit."

Jason's mother was a plump woman in early fifties, with dark blond hair worn up in a bun on the top of her head. She had bright blue eyes and a lovely clear complexion. She was dressed in a drab brown dress covered with an ash gray apron a sign of her mourning.

She led the way into the living room. I was surprised we did not go into the kitchen, as most families would have.

Beside me I sensed Jason tense as he walked through the formal room into the kitchen and took his usual seat at the table. It was cold and dark in the house.

"What. Jason is here?" asked a deep voice that cracked on the last word. Ethan walked into the kitchen.

I was shocked and dismayed upon seeing him. He was gaunt and haggard. He had grown a lot in the last month, since the funeral, but it looked like he hadn't eaten or bathed since then. His hair lay flat against his scalp and his pallor was gray. His aura was a sickly yellow-green edged with an almost black purple. He was in a deep depression.

"Ethan, it's good to see you,. How are you?" asked Jason as he rose to wrap his arms around his younger brother in a hug.

I noticed that Ethan did not return the embrace but stood there like a stone statue. I could tell Jason was struggling to cover his shock of seeing his brother in this condition.

"Well, I'm glad you could still find the place," said Ethan, glaring at Jason with hatred in his eyes.

"What?" Jason stood looking at Ethan and then at his mother.

"How am I? My life and dreams are over. That's how I am," said Ethan his eyes hard and his lips pressed together in anger.

"Ethan, don't talk like that," his mother said, as she busied herself with getting the cups and saucers out of the cupboards.

"When Dad died, I had to quit school. Now I'm trying to keep a roof over our heads and raise sheep." Ethan's voice was edged with bitterness.

"Why didn't you tell me? I thought that you and dad had hired men to help and the farm was doing well," Jason asked looking at his mother.

"It's fine. I can make it work. He would only have gone to school another two years anyway. You have your life and a new job, you couldn't leave to come home," his mother said dabbing at her eyes with a handkerchief.

Gwen and I stood watching and listening to everything in silence. This was a tough homecoming for Jason, something I was certain he never expected.

"If I had known, I would have come home sooner. You know that Ethan," said Jason, his eyes intent on his brother.

The boys glared at each other until Ethan finally nodded, his jaw firm. "I know. That's why I made mother promise not to tell you."

His mother lit the kitchen stove and lamps as we sat down in the kitchen.

Gwen and I joined Jason choosing chairs to sit in at the table. Soon we were talking about the Royal Nesting aerie, the neighbors, and Graybill's forest. It didn't seem as if Ethan was hiding anything, but I was certain he wasn't telling us everything either.

***

We said a quick hello at our home to mother, with the promise we would be back this evening, and dropped off our packs.

Soon we were entering the Jay and Otter Public House.

It was a homey pub, constructed with a lot of dark woods, the floors made of wide oak planks with rough wooden tables and chairs gathered around a central wood-burning stove. It had a high white ceiling with dark exposed beams and numerous stuffed heads of deer, elk, bears, and mountain lions decorated the walls.

"Hi there, Manny," Jason said greeting the bar keep with a nod. "We'll have three of your lagers, two chicken pies, and one beef pie."

"Good to see you Jason, Gwen, Sofia," said Manny. Gwen and I went to sit at a table while Jason walked to stand at the bar.

Manny set our drinks on the bar. "What brings you into town?" he asked.

"We came for a quick visit with the folks," Jason said then took the beverages from Manny and set them on the table in front of us then sat in an empty across from me.

I nursed my drink. I didn't like beer and planned to order a glass of water when Manny came for the second round.

Manny soon appeared with our steaming fragrant pies. I hadn't realized how hungry I was until now. "Here you go, three of the best lunches anywhere. Is there anything else I can get for you?" Manny asked, but wasn't expecting an answer since he had already turned away to greet another customer entering the pub.

"Actually, Manny," I said managing to get his attention so he turned back to face the table. I grinned.

"Two things. I'd like a glass of water; also we heard that strange things were happening in Graybill's Forest. One of the lads was talking about there being something odd going on with the Royal Nest. Have you heard anything? Seen anything?" I asked as I broke apart my pie with a crunch of pastry and watched the steam drift up to the ceiling. The smell of the herbs, vegetables, and fresh chicken smelled delicious.

Manny shrugged. "No, not really, except that your dad passed away out there. Sorry, Jason. How's your mum and brother?" asked Manny looking only at Jason avoiding eye contact with Gwen and me.

"Thanks, Manny. Mom and Ethan are getting by, but it's hard," said Jason as he took a deep drink.

We had a quick lunch, since we wanted to make it up to the Royal Nest and back down before darkness fell.

I listened to the talk around us and waited for a while. The conversations around us were strange, guarded. It was almost as if they were afraid of something. The other people in the pub had heard our conversation with Manny, they had time to talk to us about it, but no one came forward. In fact no one would even look at us.

***

We went home to change and switched to warmer layers of wool sweaters and put our hiking boots on. We had planned on going along the common trails not having to climb the jagged rocks that dotted the landscape.

It was cold and grew colder as we climbed higher on the trail. It was a good thing that we were mostly in the sunlight.

Every time we entered the shadows of the trees or giant boulders lining the path we felt the cold creep under our clothing and it chilled us to the bone.

It was a cold, but lovely hike on a beautiful winters day, but we didn't see anything unusual. We did go to the bottom of the Nest and saw that there were lots of loose rocks and boulder scattered around. This was very unusual but there was nothing that gave us an idea of how they got there.

The hike took us hours and it was twilight by the time we got back into town.

We found Ethan waiting for us at our home.

"I need to talk to you, Jason," said Ethan. His eyes were bloodshot and he was sniffling.

I could see and feel the wave of despair emanating from him. He was angry and hurt.

"You asked about things happening in Graybill's Forest in town? Did anyone say anything?"

"No, they didn't. No one is coming forward. It's as if they're afraid of something. Do you know what it is?" I asked.

"Let's go into the living room." Gwen said and led the way.

I watched him tense then he followed Gwen. He looked around my parent's living room with its deep red sofa and chairs. The fireplace was lighted and so were a pair of oil lamps on the tables next to the chairs. The mantel over the fireplace had family pictures and a few decorative ornaments on it.

We waited. Mother must have lit the fire, it cast a warm glow over everything and the pop and hiss of the logs burning gave it a cozy sound.

"Let's sit down," I suggested hoping Ethan would relax.

Ethan eyed Jason. I almost told them Gwen and I would leave the room, when I saw a change in Ethan's face and aura. The colors changed from anger and hatred to acceptance and terrible grief.

Glancing at Gwen and seeing she agreed with me I resolved to intervene. "Ethan, whatever is bothering you, Gwen and I can help. But first we have to know what's troubling you."

Ethan looked at Jason. "It's my fault. Forgive me, Jason, I killed our father." He began to sob, pouring out an uncontrollable wave of grief.

My heart ached upon hearing him and seeing him in such a state.

"Ethan, what ever happened, I'm sure it's not true. You have to be mistaken. I heard it was an accident. An avalanche."

"No, it wasn't. That's what mother told me to say, but many people know the truth. I killed him," Ethan raised his voice, becoming more agitated.

Suddenly I noticed small things in the room were beginning to move. The pictures on the mantel were starting to lift into the air then settle back into place.

"Why don't you tell us everything that happened?" I suggested glancing over at Gwen hoping she would send Ethan healing energy to calm him.

"They're all afraid of me. Afraid of what I might do to them or their families," mumbled Ethan as he stared at the flames dancing in the fireplace then looked down at the floor. His shoulder slumped forward as if he had completely given up.

I looked at Gwen and she nodded and closed her eyes. I knew that she was concentrating on sending Ethan energy.

I looked at Jason and could see the fear in his eyes. Fear for us, fear for his mother and brother.

I took in a deep breath.

"How long have you had the ability to move things?" I asked Ethan calmly. He avoided looking at me and I knew if Ethan was willing to look at me there might be hope for him.

I watched as he slowly raised his head and turn toward me. There was such a naked need for understanding in his eyes I could have wept.

"You aren't afraid?" His tone was one of bewilderment.

I stood firm in my conviction. "Perhaps a little afraid of your untrained gift, but not of you. Why don't you take your time and tell us about it?"

Ethan looked at his brother Jason nodded his encouragement.

"It was my fault. I had been having trouble at school. There was a girl in school she sat next to me. Do you remember, Luann?"

I indicated I did, I knew Luann well, but remained silent.

He became more agitated. "She hates me. I don't know why, I don't know what I did. But she lies and makes jokes about me. Everyone is laughing at me and I can't do anything about it. Dad said he'd go to school with me and talk to her, or the teachers, whatever we needed to do. He didn't get it!" Ethan began speaking louder and louder until now he was yelling.

Spittle formed at the corners of his mouth and his eyes were wide and glowing. Small objects in the room were now whirling around us, faster and faster.

"Ethan. We're listening. You love her don't you?" I understood how much it could hurt when you loved someone and all they did was laugh at you.

Ethan looked at me with horror in his eyes. Then his face softened and it slowly changed to sadness. He nodded.

"I go to Graybill's Forest when I was angry. I started to move things at home, but when I was really upset I couldn't control it. So to make sure I wouldn't hurt anyone I went to the Royal Nest, since it is completely empty most of the time.

"Except this time it wasn't, was it?" Gwen asked.

Ethan shook his head. "No, it was early evening. Dad decided to hunt some wild ewes. He's been doing this for the last few years, breeding them, keeping half the young then turning the others loose. It's helped strengthen our herd."

I nodded to encourage him to continue. He shifted his gaze to the fire.

"I didn't know!" he cried out, his anguish palatable. "I focused my energies on one side of the cliffs. I had only ever tried using my energy on bushes or trees, moving them, bursting them apart, or floating and making them glow."

Now I understood what kind of ghost we were dealing with and knew we would be able to help the Queen after all. But first we had to save Ethan.

"I deserve to die for what I did," he said at last.

Ethan looked down at the floor and I felt the power emanating from him change. The floating objects suddenly dropped as if wires suspending them had been cut. Ethan's hands started to become translucent and glowed with an eerie light.

"Ethan, I need you to look at me." I kept my voice calm and as soothing as possible.

"You can't help me," he whispered.

"Perhaps I can. But most of it will have to come from you." I felt his attention being drawn to me.

His hands stopped glowing but I could still see through them.

"Breath. Take a deep breath in and then slowly release it."

He turned toward me and I slowly exhaled, paused, and then inhaled. I repeated my breathing encouraging Ethan to follow my rhythm.

"Ethan, what happened with father was an accident. If you intended it, you wouldn't be feeling this way. You have a gift, a very powerful one," Jason said.

Ethan looked at his brother, a small glimmer of hope in his eyes.

"It will take time to control your gift, but we know a school that will train you. It's close to the castle. You can stay with Sofia and me when we get married," offered Jason.

I held my breath hoping Ethan would accept the offer.

"Mother?" He asked anxiously.

"She'll be fine. I'm sure she would love to come to live in Umber and stay with her sister. Or she could decide to keep farming sheep here. We'll let her decide with our help and support," Jason assured his brother.

Ethan nodded and gave us all a tentative smile as his eyes filled with tears of relief.

"First we will need you to come with us to see the Queen. We'll start work on your control and safe ways of releasing energy on the way back to Umber," said Gwen.

"Do we want to go to your home, Ethan, to talk to your mother tonight? Then we can all go home tomorrow?" I asked the group.

All three heads nodded in unison.

"Good," I said, "and the following day we will fully explain to the Queen about the ghosts in the Royal Nest and the Forest of Graybill's King."

The Queen, and the King, would be pleased and we were pleased that we would be able to go home with the quest resolved.

The future would hold other quests for us. Gwen, Jason, and I were now heroes of the Kingdom.

Three Sisters

Murder driven by greed to gain a valuable inheritance, but who's behind the murderous plot to jump the family succession?

A SOFT, FOAM rubber ball struck her on the left side of her head. Rebecca snagged it in midair as she flipped her shoulder-length, brown streaked with silver hair over her shoulders, then lobbed the spongy ball back at Wayne, her twenty-five-year-old youngest son.

"Really? In the kitchen, Wayne?"

The kitchen had clean lines of glass, stainless steel, and marble. She grabbed a large mug of coffee from the counter. The panoramic view through the floor to ceiling windows was of forest, fields, and the ocean beyond. North Vancouver was lovely any time of year.

The back door swung open admitting Rupert, her husband of thirty years, and running after him were two large, longhaired red dogs, both barking and wagging their tails. The stink of wet dog permeated the room. Rupert cocked his head as he looked at her.

"What's the matter, who died?" asked Wayne and Rupert as one.

She paused before she replied, seeing the look of horror appear on their faces as they understood they had been correct in their quip. Their timing and humor had utterly failed.

"Aunt Bernice passed away this morning. I have to go over and do damage control. Are you coming?" She looked at Rupert, who nodded, then she turned to run up the staircase.

Rebecca knew she'd have to change into a proper mourning suit before she went to the Simmons' estate. She walked up the stairs, her mind whirling with all the things that would need to be done.

First, retrieve her aunt's Last Will and Testament from the office. She turned down the hall, rounding the corner to enter her own office. The smell of lavender greeted her. The cream-colored floor, warm oak furniture, and slate-blue walls created a calmness and warmth that affected her every time she came into the room.

She pulled out the copy of her aunt's will from the file cabinet behind her desk. She had it on file, since she was the executor. Odd it wasn't filed properly; it was in the Three Sisters company file folder and not the personal folder for Bernice Simmons.

Damn, she was right. It wasn't an original; it couldn't be admitted in court.

"Ready, honey, let's go," said Rupert, coming into her office after changing.

He was a handsome man, still slender even though he was in his fifties, with dark brown hair, clean-shaven, with hazel-green eyes. Rebecca felt herself drawn to Rupert even after their thirty years together.

She felt a seductive smile cross her face as she stepped toward him, her arms reaching out for him.

"Come on, we'll have to do something about that thought of yours later, not now."

She nodded, waving the will at him. "We've got problems. This isn't an original, so it's no good; and it wasn't in its place in the files."

Rupert's eyebrows rose at the last comment. He knew she was beyond particular about where she put things; no one touched her files except her.

"Someone was in our home and in those files. That means we have a much bigger problem than an estate," she eyed her husband. "It's a very big estate and that doesn't take into account Three Sisters Inc.. The sisters' company has a massive portfolio. It was started by my mothers father for her and her two other sisters. He was determined that his daughters would have money of their own and never need to beg their husbands for a 'hand out' as he used to put it. It had been directed by my grandfather and now it a good portion of my work as well putting my MBA and love of investments to good use.

"Aunt Bernice just had a full battery of tests and was in wonderful health according to her new doctor. That being the case, we'll have to determine if Aunt Bernice died of natural causes or was murdered. We better take a look at the will so I can make a list of suspects. If we follow the money, we'll have a short list."

"Come on, Rebecca, I think you're jumping to conclusions. We don't know if anything is wrong."

"I do know, but we'll deal with this one careful step at a time. Today is Monday. We leave for Brussels next Friday. We'll have a graveside funeral this Friday and the memorial service on Wednesday, next week. I'll have to contact the Three Sisters, the sisters' company. As far as I know, the administrator is still the same."

Rupert shrugged and smiled.

Rebecca looked at her husband and smiled back. She watched a shudder go through his body.

He went to get the car and bring it round front as she loaded the documents into her leather briefcase. Before she left, she put on a black bowler hat with a short black veil. She freshened her grapefruit-tasting lipstick, smiled to herself, and nodded.

Now she was ready.

She wore her preferred sleek navy pantsuit with a heavy cream-colored silk sweater underneath. Her favorite flat Barneys on her feet, a cross-body Burberry bag on her shoulder, with her Royce soft-sided black briefcase in her hand. *I'm such a fashionista.*

Rupert pulled up in the family's steel-gray Jaguar XF Portfolio. She slid into the passenger side, then rolled down the window. Tension melted from her body as she relaxed, letting the cool spring air, smelling of wet earth and growing things, swirl around her face. Her gray eyes softened as she thought of her aunt.

"Once we get to Aunt Bernice's, we need to take a good look at her room to check her safe for the current will, if Miss Kirsch hasn't found it yet," she said.

"You really don't like her very much, do you?"

Rebecca shook her head. "No, not really. I always thought Aunt Bernice could have found a better assistant than her, that's all."

They cranked up the volume on the car radio and listened to some good tunes without saying anything. The last song finished; the news came on. A somber announcer started speaking. "We are sad to announce Mrs. Bernice Simmons, a great philanthropist and someone who will be missed by many in this community, has passed away. She was found this morning by her assistant, Miss Alex Kirsch, who gave us an exclusive interview."

Rebecca clenched her jaw as she pressed her lips together in anger. She switched off the radio.

"Darling, calm yourself. We'll be there in a few minutes."

"I guess that's why she couldn't meet me at the house. She asked me to meet her at the Vancouver Fairmont Hotel for lunch. I specifically told her not to talk to anyone, especially the press. Obviously, she ignored me."

They arrived at the estate. Rebecca was out of the vehicle before Rupert put the car into park. She grabbed her things, moved to the front door where she flung it open, then marched into the foyer.

Stanley, the long-time butler, greeted them at the front door. "Mrs. Rebecca, it's so good of you to come."

"Good morning, Stanley, forgive my intrusion, but...."

"Yes, we heard Miss Kirsch on the radio a few minutes ago." His thin, bloodless lips formed a tight line.

"Please take me up to Aunt Bernice's room. Is the doctor still here?"

"Yes. Follow me."

Rupert walked into the house to join her and they followed Stanley up the expansive staircase and into Aunt Bernice's room. Rebecca wanted to run into the bedroom, hoping to find her aunt alive. She knew it was foolish.

"Stanley, please call the police," Rebecca asked as they reached Aunt Bernice's room.

"Certainly." Stanley turned and walked downstairs.

"What are you doing? Stop that. You can't break into her safe." Shouts of indignation were erupting from the bedroom. Rebecca and Rupert rushed into the room to find the doctor wrestling with a woman in her thirties.

"All right, that's enough. Kirsch, let the doctor go!" Rebecca shouted. They immediately stopped their struggling, staring incredulously at the new arrivals.

Rebecca moved toward them but Rupert grabbed her shoulder and pulled her back behind him. Then she noticed the black pistol in Kirsch's hand.

"What the hell do you think you're doing?" Rebecca stepped around Rupert. "Drop that gun before you hurt yourself."

"I know how to use this." Waving the gun at them, Miss Kirsch stepped away from the doctor lying on the floor. "I'm defending what belonged to Mrs. Simmons. I'm not going to let this man steal her things."

The doctor raised from the floor, his black eyes on Rupert, then Rebecca.

"Please explain yourselves," Rebecca said as she entered the room.

She noticed a painting had been moved exposing the wall safe, but it was still closed.

"He came in here and was trying to open it," said Kirsch, a woman in her thirties, still pointing the gun at them. She wore her red hair short, her emerald-green eyes were intense, and there was a curious little scar between her nose and her bottom lip.

"Oh, for pity's sake, I told Aunt Bernice not to give you a gun and teach you to shoot." Rebecca strode forward and took the gun out of Kirsch's hand, then handed it to Rupert.

"Okay, Doctor, why were you trying to get into the safe?"

Before responding, the doctor brushed off his pants and smoothed his hair back on his head with long slender fingers "I wasn't. I came in and found this woman trying to get into it. I tried to stop her, not the other way around."

"Your turn," Rebecca said to Kirsch.

"I have a right to be here, to what's in her safe. You told me to search for her will." Kirsch spoke angrily.

"I asked you to check the files, not the safe. I also said not to speak to anyone, especially the reporters. Do you normally pick and choose what you do?" She took a deep, steadying breath. "All right, let's all calm down."

Rebecca motioned for everyone to sit in one of several wing chairs in the large bedroom, then quickly went to the powder room off the bedroom.

When Rebecca returned, she paced off the distance between the wall with the safe and the powder room, two times, before she sat.

Rebecca requested the doctor run some simple tests on her aunt to confirm her death was of natural causes. Bernice was a very healthy, active woman in her late eighties and she wanted to know how her aunt had died.

Rebecca stood and went to the safe, putting her body between the others and the safe to block their view. Knowing the combination, she opened it.

The safe was empty.

"You knew the combination? She never told it to me," Kirsch complained, her tone spiteful.

Rebecca looked to Rupert. "Come here a minute, please. And put the gun in the nightstand where it belongs. As a kid I'd heard a rumor that there was a secret safe in this room, but of course I didn't believe it. But it was just an old story or was it?"

Rupert did as she requested. "Touch this wall." He did. "Good; now go to the door of the powder room and look at the wall behind the door. How long should that wall be?"

Kirsch slowly went to the side of the large bed, then stopped, waiting.

"Okay, how do we get in?" Rupert asked as he smiled at Rebecca.

A loud, measured ticking sound started, gradually getting louder and faster.

Rebecca's heart rate increased. She knew what the sound was immediately even though she had never really heard one before.

"Bomb! Get out!"

The doctor and Kirsch did as they were told and ran out the bedroom door. Rupert stayed to watch Rebecca.

Rebecca ran back to the safe and slammed it closed. The ticking stopped. She then turned the handle like a doorknob. A panel slid open to the right of the safe. It blended in so well with the wall, no one would have ever known that there was a door there.

"The wall safe was a decoy. She needed more room for her valuables. This may be where a real copy of the newest will is located," said Rebecca.

"Well, can you see it?" asked Kirsch, looking into the safe-room from the doorway, her gray eyes curious.

"Actually, I think it best for you and the doctor to leave this room now. As executor, I'll check the will."

"Rupert, could you please make sure that Kirsch leaves the room. The police should be here soon, maybe they'd like to talk to her?"

Rupert nodded and went out of the room. Soon Rebecca heard loud voices, then a door being closed, then he was back.

Rebecca walked to a small wooden filling cabinet, slid open the first drawer, and started her search.

Rebecca scanned the small safe-room. It was a basic room, five feet by ten feet; there was a very small teak desk in one corner facing into the room, with a leather ergonomic office chair. The only other furniture was a slim red upholstered recliner, a small gray loveseat, and teak side and coffee tables.

It seemed Aunt Bernice liked things in threes: there were three breathtaking paintings on the walls, three beautiful antique swords, three sculptures, and seating for three.

Rupert stayed by the door, acting as lookout.

He watched her methodically go through each drawer as she quickly flipped through the contents and files.

"How are you doing, Rebecca?" asked Rupert after a few minutes.

"Fine. I have what we came for." She triumphantly held up an envelope and a file folder.

Rebecca heard a noise. The door started to slide closed. "Rupert!" shouted Rebecca, "We have to go. Now!"

Rupert placed both hands on the doorframe and pulled hard, trying to stop it from closing. Rebecca sprinted toward the opening and dashed through, giving Rupert time to pivot past the edge of the door and into the bedroom. It closed behind them with a dull *thud*.

"Okay, let's go. I want a few words with Kirsch and the doctor before we leave. I need to get downtown to Aunt Bernice's bank and talk to the administrator at Three Sisters."

"Fine, I'll cover your back," said Rupert, following Rebecca down the stairs.

"Stanley, may I speak with you?"

Stanley popped out of the hallway. "I'm here, Mrs. Rebecca. How may I serve you?"

"Oh yes, very good, Stanley. Could you please call everyone to the library for me in about ten minutes? I'd like to speak to everyone and reassure them."

"Very well, Miss, I'll call them together." He bowed from the waist.

"Miss Kirsch, could I see you in the day room, please," said Rebecca as she turned and went into the cozy day room, decorated in mustard yellows and ocean blues. She looked out at the back garden through the expansive window overlooking the vast yard beyond.

"Yes?" Kirsch stood tall, a scowl darkening her narrow face, glaring at Rebecca.

"This morning, before I came here, I was going to offer you the administrator position of the estate. But with your attitude and actions, I need you to give me your house keys." Rebecca held out her hand. Kirsch pulled her keys from her pocket, then threw them at her and stormed away.

"Stanley will help you pack some of your things. You may make arrangements to pick up the remainder of your possessions," said Rebecca to Kirsch's retreating back. She watched Stanley follow her up the stairs until they disappeared from view.

Rebecca entered the library to alleviate the fears of the staff; they would all keep their jobs. The estate would continue because it would take years for the will to be executed.

As Rebecca left the house, she checked her cell phone for any messages. There were more than she could count. She'd deal with them on the way into the city.

"I'm going to need about an hour or so in town. How about you?" she said as she and Rupert started walking to the car. Tall fir and cedar trees lined the circular driveway but the centerpiece was the classical water fountain surrounded by palm trees. It was an interesting contrast of nature.

Quirky, just like Aunt Bernice. A lump developed in her throat. Suppressing the urge to weep, she knew she'd have time to grieve later.

"Miss Rebecca, a word before you go, please?" said Stanley at the front door as they walked past him. Kirsch walked past them without a word, avoiding looking at them. The former secretary had a loaded suitcase that she dragged at her side and matching suit bags hanging from her shoulders.

They watched as she left the estate on foot.

"Yes, Stanley, I'm happy to talk to you. For now, I'd like you to take care of the estate and I'm naming you the administrator, effective immediately. If Kirsch comes back, it is you, and only you, she'll meet with. She is not to take any electronics with her. Even her personal computer stays here until I personally release it."

Stanley's eyes shone and he gave a little bow. "Thank you. I have already seen to the computer. She didn't take anything she didn't arrive with, including her computer and cell phone."

"Very nicely done. If you need me, call. Here's my private number." She handed him a business card. He nodded and smiled.

"Thank you very much, Miss Rebecca. Let me know what you need and how I may serve."

Rebecca adjusted her purse strap on her shoulder and gripped her briefcase.

Rupert pulled his car keys from his pants pocket, then unlocked the doors with the remote. His thumb pressed the starter button on the remote and immediately there was a resounding explosion, the force of which knocked them to the ground. The car was a smoking ruin, with flames pouring from the shattered metal and plastics.

"Are you okay?" shouted an anxious Stanley as he ran toward them.

"Yes, I'm fine," said Rebecca after running her hands down her body. "Rupert?"

"Yeah, a little shook up, but still in one piece. We'll need another car," suggested Rupert.

"Of course. Shall I call Jonathan?" Stanley asked. Jonathan had been her late aunt's driver. "Or would you prefer to use the RAV4?"

"The RAV4 would be ideal," said Rupert, helping Rebecca to stand.

"Excellent choice." Stanley raised a cell phone to his ear, instructing a staff member inside to bring them the Toyota SUV.

"I have also called the police about the car bomb. Another thing I wanted to mention to you, the man you kept calling doctor isn't Madam's doctor. The doctor was here when you arrived, but left soon after. Here is his number."

"Then who is he?" asked Rebecca. Stanley shrugged his shoulders but didn't answer her.

"Please tell the police that we will be pleased to answer any questions they have and give them my private number."

From around the corner of the manor house, their ride appeared. The car was a nice little cream RAV4 Limited. Rebecca looked at Rupert, who accepted the keys from the driver.

"Well, this certainly brings back memories," she said as she settled into the passenger's seat.

"Yup, if I remember, this is just like your little *baby,* isn't it? I fought that car for your attention, and I won."

Once inside, Rupert shifted the car into drive and headed into downtown.

They arrived at the bank first. The manager met them and verified Rebecca was indeed the executor for the estate. Next, she went to the offices of Three Sisters to meet with Bob Adams, her aunt's administrator. As they walked into the building, she saw the so-called doctor, seated in one of the nearby offices.

They walked into Bob's office, a large airy space with a round walnut table at one end and a matching desk, visitor's chairs, and a sofa in the other. A row of windows overlooked the paved parking lot.

He quietly closed the door behind them. Rebecca was ready for anything: fight, flight, or coffee.

She'd known Bob for a long time, but at this stage in the game, she wasn't sure what was going on or whom to trust.

"Bob, that man in the other office. Who is he and why was he at Aunt Bernice's estate today?"

"Ah, yes. First let me say I will miss Bernice Simmons very, very much. We had a good, profitable relationship together over the last forty years. As for who that man is, his name is Miles Reed." Bob paused and looked intently at Rebecca before he continued. "He's one of our young executives. He came to my attention about five years ago and I've been grooming him to succeed me ever since."

"Succeed you? I agree with the idea it's always good to make succession plans, but what are you really saying, Bob? You're thinking of retiring? And you still haven't told me what he was doing at the house."

"Yes, let's talk about Miles. Because of the succession planning, I asked him to go to see your aunt about her will, to make sure we had an up-to-date copy. As you know, the Three Sisters was founded by the father of your three aunts. They each receive a percentage of the proceeds of the company every year while the rest remains invested. Over the last seventy years, it has grown and diversified into a very big conglomerate."

"Aunt Alice, my third aunt is still living, and when she passes, the entire company will be collapsed and the proceeds will go to a combination of trusts and charities." Rebecca pulled out her cell phone and checked it. She was waiting to hear the results of the first round of tests from the coroner. She noticed that there was a call from the police asking she contact them.

"I'm sorry, Bob. I need to make a quick call." She contacted the police and they notified her that her Aunt Alice had passed away yesterday. Her eyes filled with alarm as she looked at Bob.

He gave her a sad smile and nodded at her. "I guess you haven't been notified yet, but your Aunt Alice died yesterday."

There was a knock and they all looked toward the door. Bob went to pull it open; Miles stood there.

"Mrs. Royal, I'm sorry for barging in like this, but I feel we need to talk. There are things you don't know."

"Okay, Bob, maybe it's best if we sit down and do some succession planning of our own." Rebecca sat in one of the two visitors chairs and Miles sat in the other.

"Bob, you were saying Miles was at the house to obtain a copy of the current will. Fine. Miles, why were you wrestling with Miss Kirsch?"

"I was successful finding a will, but I don't think it's the most current. But I hope you're having the doctor do a post mortem on Mrs. Simmons. I believe she was poisoned. And I suspect Miss Kirsch murdered her."

"Fine. Why didn't you correct me when I called you doctor?" said Rebecca, leaning back in the leather executive chair.

"For two reasons. First, that would lead to a lot of questions I didn't want to answer, and second, I really didn't have time to. With everything that happened—the death, the gun, the safe, and the bomb—the house was in chaos. Then you told us all to leave. I did. I brought with me the copy of the will I found and reported back to Mr. Adams."

Suddenly screaming started in the reception area outside Bob's office door. They looked at each other and stood up as one.

"Where is he? Where is Miles, that killer!" It was a woman's voice. The screaming grew louder and louder. The door suddenly burst open and there stood Kirsch.

"There he is. He killed Mrs. Simmons! He's the one! He poisoned her, it was so fast. What did you use Cyanide? He said he was going to blame me." She sobbed hysterically. Her eyes were black holes and her lipstick was smeared over her chin.

Rebecca drew in a sharp breath.

The crying Kirsch held a grenade in her right hand.

"This was my father's and I'm going to use it. I'm not going to go to prison for something I didn't do. My life is over and so is yours." The fingers of her left hand grasped the arming pin on the deadly weapon.

Rebecca leapt forward to tackle Kirsch. They fell to the floor in a heap of tangled limbs, but Rebecca managed to wrestle the grenade from the crazed woman. But in the struggle, Kirsch had already pulled the arming pin.

Rebecca grabbed the bomb, turned, and threw it out the office window into the parking lot. The grenade blew up, shattering the windows.

A tall, muscular male security guard appeared in the front office. The guard helped Kirsch from the floor, gripping her right arm and lifting her to her feet. He then secured her wrists in handcuffs. Kirsch avoided looking at them, her eyes wet with tears.

Bob looked at Rebecca and nodded. "I'll call the police," said Bob.

Once the office was cleared, Rebecca pulled her cell from her purse. She made a quick call to the coroner's office.

"That was the coroner's office. Aunt Bernice was murdered with an overdose of digitalis. They suspect it was in her tea."

She pulled out an envelope. "This is the will, Bob. As you know, I'm named as executor and you as second executor if needed.

"The estate is going to take years to unravel, because I think we're going to have to wait for a murder trial first. I also know Miss Alex Kirsch was looking at you and not at Miles when she accused you of murder."

Rebecca stood up and opened the office door and two police detectives waited in the outer office. "Gentlemen, you may want to come in and question Mr. Robert Adams. I believe he has a lot of answers for you."

One Day At A Time

*When the end of the world seems imminent people are willing to
make extraordinary sacrifices for others.*

ELLEN STOOD on her long, wide, back deck facing the inlet. She
was wearing her purple fleece nightgown and holding a steaming cup
of coffee, looking out at the water.

It was such a mild morning on the Sunshine Coast on this first
week of January; she couldn't believe how fortunate they were this
year. It seemed that they had escaped any snow at all.

They'd only had a few cold days of below freezing at night, just
enough to set her spring-flowering bulbs. She looked over at the side
yard at the buds on her magnolia that were swelling and the roses
that she had planted last summer; they had still been in bloom only
four weeks ago.

Then her eyes glanced at the lads, their dogs, playing tag in the
backyard. One, Samson, a seven-year-old golden retriever, and the
other a small, fourteen-year-old red terrier, Rusty.

The heavy rains they'd had for the last two week had stopped so
today would be a good day to stretch their legs. They all needed a
walk.

She looked back out at the water. She never tired of looking at
the keyhole view they had of the Georgia Straight, the stretch of
water between themselves and Vancouver Island.

A well-seasoned sailboat captain had told her that there were only about eight miles of water between Gibsons and the large island. All she knew was when she and Lee, her husband of twenty-five years, had seen this little two-story home with its level entry and walkout basement, they knew they had found home.

There was lots of room for family and guests, and the tall evergreen and arbutus trees that surrounded it made if feel cozy, their little cabin in the woods.

As she watched the water, she realized that something was wrong.

In all the time they had lived here, you could get to the water by walking a long set of wooden stairs. Ellen leaned over the railing and looked at the waves between the trees on the right side of her view. The waves were coming from the west. Usually that meant fair weather, but something stank, really badly. It wasn't the pulp mill; they got the odd smell from there a couple of times a year. No, this was like Oyster Bay at very low tide: mud, dead shellfish, oysters, muscles, and seaweed. It made you want to heave.

She had never, ever, no matter how low the tide got, seen the bottom. There was always water covering the rocks and gravel directly below them, but not this morning.

She'd left the television on when she checked the weather station and now she heard the emergency signal. At least that's what she thought it was. She called to the dogs as she went back into the house and looked at the large television in the corner of the living room between the bay window and the built-in mantle over the wood-burning fireplace.

She heard Matthew, her three-year-old grandson, getting up and coming into the living room and gave him a quick smile.

"Honey, why don't you go and find Grandpa? Tell him I want to see him right now. Hurry please," she said. She tried to emphasize the words without scaring Matthew. The boy scooted away as the announcer came on.

"A comet hit the Pacific Ocean this morning. We are expecting earthquakes in the next few minutes and tidal waves to batter the Pacific Northwest this late morning, especially the area from San Francisco to Canada," said a man who could barely contain his fear.

Ellen quickly turned off the television in case Mathew heard what was happening. She looked to the telephone. Should she try and call Mathew's parents? She had to at least try. Then she'd make a quick call to her other son, too. She picked up the cordless phone and started to dial. All she got was a busy signal even before she finished the phone number. She put the phone down on the kitchen counter.

Oh God, please not that.

She had heard so much about tsunamis from her friends in Oregon, all she could do was repeat what they had said to her over and over again. *Get to higher ground. Get to higher ground.* It was a litany that kept repeating in her head. Ellen felt herself start to panic and then her rational brain kicked in. *You can panic later, but right now you need to act.*

"Lee, I need you to come up right now! I mean *right now*!" she called down to the basement. She hoped he heard her, he had to come now.

They had at most five minutes to leave and get to higher ground. She checked her watch. *Okay go.*

Once the earthquakes started, there was no telling how the roads around her would hold up and they had to get out before the tidal wave.

What do you need? And I mean need? She thought to herself as she went through her list of must-have things.

She ran into the guest bedroom and grabbed a large, wheeled backpack. She was like a madwoman as she ran through the house, opening drawers. Grabbing three of things for each of them: three socks and underwear, three tee shirts, three pants, a pair of running shoes and hiking boots. She grabbed the dog bowls, their kibble—luckily they had just gotten more the other day—and their treats.

They had to get out of here. *Don't dawdle*, she thought as she ran into the living room and grabbed the photos and albums off the mantle and the antique oak, mirrored hutch.

The best place would be the Safeway parking lot at the junction of Pratt and Gibsons Road. It was very high ground and she knew that this whole area was on a massive granite vein of rock that stretched for about one hundred miles all down the coast.

The dogs came bounding into the house, barking, happy to be able to play without the benefit of the dark days and heavy rains that they had been having, which was typical of a winter in Gibsons.

She ran and closed the sliding glass patio door so the dogs couldn't get out.

"Lee, I need you here right now!" Ellen yelled, all pretense of niceness gone. She tried to weight the odds of how many people would be trying to get to Safeway to find safety and food and water.

She heard the basement door open and Mathew's light, little-boy's voice chatting to his grandfather as they came up the stairs.

"What's the problem Ellen? We're coming," he said as he walked up the stairs with her bulging laptop bag in his hand. He looked over the banister and saw her dragging the case with their clothes to the front door.

He took one look at her and quickly walked to her side and put an arm around her. "What is it, one of the kids?" he asked softly in her ear.

"No, worse—much worse. A comet has hit the Pacific Ocean; there's going to be tidal waves and earthquakes. They're talking like the San Andreas Fault is finally going to let loose, too," said Ellen as she watched Lee's eyes get softer. She spoke so fast most people would not be able to understand her. Then he looked around the foyer and by the front door, licked his lips, and nodded.

"Okay. I've got my laptop and the mini tower," he said as he walked into their pantry, pulled out a large cloth shopping bag, then went down the hall and pulled down three of his favorite paintings that she had done over the years.

"We need to get to higher ground right now," they said in unison.

"They said they don't know when things are going to happen, but I figure we've got five minutes. Listen carefully," she said looking at her wristwatch. "We've used three of them already."

She quickly went through the things she had packed, from flashlights with extra batteries to toilet paper and everything in between. He listened as she spoke and they started to carry things that they would be taking with them to their tan-colored RAV4.

"Can you think of anything else? I don't have much fresh water, so I used some of our buckets and a couple of pots with tap water that we can use when we get home. I filled a few plastic bottles for our trip now . I'm hoping to get some more water at the grocery store. It's better to have more than not enough." Ellen had to stop for a minute. She was breathing so hard and her mouth was so dry that she was starting to get dizzy.

Lee put his arms around her and held her. "It's going to be okay. We have Vancouver Island to take the brunt of the tidal action. And as for earthquakes, as you told me when we bought the house: the huge granite vein under us and Mt. Capstone behind us has stood for many years and will be here for a very long time to come. We'll see how the house and your studio do," he laughed softly as he gently pushed her short, dark brown hair from her face and kissed her forehead.

They looked at each other, nodded, and quickly pulled the rest of the things out of the front door and into the back of the RAV4.

In Ellen's head, she kept on hearing, *get to higher ground, get to higher ground.* "We are, we are," she mumbled under her breath to herself.

Lee picked up Mathew, strapped him into his car seat in the back, and Ellen, armed with a pocket full of dog treats, grabbed Rusty and threw him in the rear seat with a treat, then grabbed Samson and put him the back seat, too.

As she was going to close the back door, Mathew started to cry and kick his feet.

"It's okay, Mathew, we're going on a car ride up to Safeway, " she said as she leaned forward and picked up a toy that had fallen onto the seat. As she did, Samson decided that he would squeeze past her and started to head up the driveway.

Ellen's heart almost stopped. She knew that Samson had been really bad lately about coming when called. She could feel her stomach clench and her mind jumped to what might happen.

She had to get him in the car. They had to leave NOW! They had to get to higher ground. Above all else they had to keep Mathew safe, and that might mean leaving Samson behind. She felt her eyes swell with tears and her vision blurred.

She prepared herself; she'd have to live with whatever happened. She only had one chance before they left.

"Okay, Sampson. Come," she said with authority.

Sampson walked to the top of the driveway and sniffed their hedge.

She shook the dog treats. "Sampson. Cookie."

The dog looked up at her and slowly wagged his tail, his tongue lolled out from the side of his mouth. Great, the dog was grinning at her, thinking it was a game.

She felt Rusty jump up onto the back seat of the RAV4. "Sampson, car ride. Cookie."

In her heart, Ellen was begging for Sampson to come. She turned her back to the dog, shook the bag of treats, and gave Rusty another cookie making sure that Sampson could see what she was doing. "Please God, please," she whispered under her breath, begging for the big dog to come.

"Get in the truck, Ellen. He's wandering down the street," said Lee in a resigned but firm voice.

She knew that she could just walk up and get him, but he was wandering too far away now. He'd gone a block and a half and they only had a few precious moments. She couldn't risk all their lives.

She closed the rear door and quickly walked around the truck and slid into the front passenger seat. She held back the tears; she would never forgive herself for leaving Samson, her big, goofy buddy. She could feel sobs fill her chest and tears fill her eyes. She looked out of the window and tried to swallow her grief.

Maybe they would find him after this was all over. He knew the area because of their walks together, and he was smart. She bet that he'd get home before they would, but her tears wouldn't stop.

"Okay let's go!" she said as she put on her seatbelt and slammed the door closed. She took a deep breath and held onto the armrest.

Lee stepped on the gas. Nothing happened. He tried again, but the car wouldn't start. Nothing. This had never happened before. He looked at Ellen. She glanced at him as she opened her door and jumped out.

"It won't start. Look, grab Mathew and start up Third Street. I'll meet you at Safeway or along the road," said Lee as he looked at Ellen.

She almost laughed at the suggestion. Yeah, she could get a short way up the hill, but not all the way to the highway; it was a good four to five miles away. Would she get there with a small three-year-old boy in tow in the next few minutes? *Not a chance.*

"Come on, get out. I'll get the car going," she said. She stood to the side and Lee jumped out. She slid behind the wheel, waved her remote control key, stepped on the brake firmly, and then hit the start button once it went green.

A welcoming deep rumble greeted their ears as the car sprang to life.

"Okay, let's try this again," said Ellen and she got back into the passenger seat.

She looked up and noticed that the steady traffic in front of their door had slowed and then stopped.

"Lee, let's go up Third and then swing up Robin. I have a feeling that the traffic is plugged on Ocean View. Besides, we'll constantly be going up and getting higher," said Ellen as she cleared her throat.

Lee checked the radio. There was only static on all the stations. He checked them all twice and nothing was on any of them, so he turned it off.

"Gram, breakfast?" asked Mathew, who had been very quiet up to now.

"Sure, how about a nice, soft, blueberry bar and some water?" Ellen asked as she pulled up the large bag of snacks, juice, and their small amount of bottled water. She opened a bar and handed it to him.

Ellen, rolled down her window. Everything was eerily quiet. No bird song, no chitterling from squirrels, no eagle's cry. She looked up. No birds; the only things moving were the trees, swaying with the wind.

"We'll go as far as we can. The Safeway lot is probably full right now. Any ideas?" asked Lee as he kept the truck steadily moving.

Suddenly the truck started to sway. A huge, sixty-foot maple tree in front of them started to lean and then fall. The crash shook the truck; luckily the tree fell away from the road. Lee stopped and waited. There were only a few cars before and behind them; they all stopped as well. They resumed crawling forward and arrived at the corner of Overlook and Proud and turned left. They had passed by the steep switchbacks and the S curves on Overlook; now the road was straight all the way up to the main highway, where the Safeway was.

They drove up Proud slowly. There were cars and trucks in the ditch, people walking up the road carrying children and belongings. They would occasionally look behind them at the water, then back toward the mountain where they were heading.

They were about a mile away from the Safeway when another earthquake hit. This time the telephone poles across the street started to fall like dominoes, along the road and not across it. They kept on moving. So far, so good.

"I don't think that we'll have much of a problem here in Gibsons. At least, not at first. The house may even remain standing. It probably won't have any glass windows left, and we won't have electricity, but I'm hoping that we still have a working septic tank— but I guess we need electricity for that and our water, don't we?"

Lee nodded as he watched the road and the other cars around him, waiting for another quake to hit them.

"I am worried about the kids, and our family and friends in Vancouver. I think some places will be fine. Don't you?"

"I'm worried, too. Look out the window, can you see the ocean from here? Maybe it won't be as bad as they predict. I'm worried about the ferries," said Lee, letting Ellen's question hang.

Ellen craned her head toward the water. "I don't see any... oh, now I see water. It's about halfway across to the island. I can't see what's happening on the other side of the island in the Long Beach area. I sure hope they get clear of all this. Mathew's asleep."

Lee nodded as they were buffeted again, this time harder, and the truck slid to the right. He stopped, waited, and then proceeded slowly.

"Sason. Sason, where is he?" asked a sleepy Mathew as he woke and stretched. He started to sniffle as he looked around. "I want Sason. Here, Sason!"

Ellen looked at Lee and saw tears in his eyes that he brushed away with the back of his hand. She swallowed hard, trying to keep herself from getting emotional. "What do I say? How do I tell him that we just left Samson?"

"It's like we said. Samson went for a walk, he's exploring, and we hope he's at home by the time we get back."

Ellen nodded and used her fingers to rub the tears from her eyes. She felt like such a failure.

She should have done something, she should have trained the dog better. But if that dog…no, *when* that dog came back, he would be so trained no one would recognize him. She'd make sure of it.

"Honey, Samson went exploring, remember? Hopefully he'll be finished and at home when we get there. Do you want some water now?" She reached back and unscrewed the cap. "Remember, only a little bit at a time."

The little boy took the bottle and she grabbed a towel and put it on his chest in case he spilt. She watched him and smiled. He was their reason to continue on. They had to protect him and make sure that he didn't just survive, but that he thrived. He was the reason they had to go to higher ground, he was the reason they would be all right.

"I was trying to think of somewhere else that we could go, in the same area. Ideas?" Lee asked.

"How about George's place? You remember the contractor who built the studio and the fences for us?"

"Yeah? Oh, the empty lots in his subdivision?" asked Lee. He smiled and nodded at Ellen.

"Yeah. If the empty lots are full of cars, maybe we can park on the street. At least for tonight? We're high enough now," said Ellen, looking back over her shoulder.

"Okay."

"I also um… have a shovel if we need to dig a hole. It will be just like camping when the kids were little, won't it?" Ellen looked at him and grinned. She remembered how much he hated camping.

"Honey, I'm afraid that we're going to have to take this one day at a time and hope for the best."

She was concerned over a lot of things: would they have water, would they have electricity, would they have help from the mainland. How many people would likely die without their medications? How many would be gone in the next three weeks, three months, six months, or a year?

Ellen stopped the racing thoughts in her mind. She had to focus on what was happening right now and deal with the problems and solutions in front of them.

She knew there were people that lived off the grid here on the Sunshine Coast, so if they had to face this crisis, this was a good place to be. Only time would tell, but right now she had to calm her mind about the what-ifs.

They reached the crossroads of the main highway and drove to the other side.

Ellen felt herself relax. They were well over the tsunami level now.

"Keep driving. I see that the Safeway is full, but I still see empty lots in George's subdivision. We're going to be okay, at least for today," Ellen said as she reached over and squeezed Lee's hand.

All they could do was do their best, and as Lee said, take it one day at a time.

Party Line

There was a time when phone lines were party lines and you could hear what your neighbor was saying. This girl hears something that terrifies her.

SHE LOOKED OUT of the curtains, first on one side of the heavily carved oak front door, then on the other side. Nothing.

It was a lovely, crisp winter's day in Vancouver. The sky was blue and the North Shore Mountains, which she could see from her front door, were a deep purple with bright white peaks. Magnificent. She paced back and forth on the glossy hardwood floors, the smell of lemon polish and beeswax light in the air, but Miss Kate Baker was oblivious to everything except for one thing.

Where was he, where was the telephone installer? She looked into the living room with its tall bay windows and deep red curtains, tied back to let in the sunlight. On the mantel sat a china clock her parents had brought back with them from Paris from their last trip.

She was right, that stupid man was late. She had told Susan she would call her on their new telephone at noon, and it was almost that time now. She heard something in the street out front. Could it be him? She didn't want to appear too anxious, but they would be the first family in South Hill to have a phone. Not just South Hill, she'd be the first at St. Mary's to have a phone.

She heard a car stop on the street outside and a door slam. She turned and ran from the foyer.

"Ruthie, get the front door. Hurry." Kate turned and ran from the foyer so the maid could answer the door.

100

***

Kate, a girl in her last year of high school, looked at the newly installed black telephone, hanging from the wall in the hall of her wide foyer. She was a tall, slender girl, pretty enough, but her eyes were a little too small, her nose a little too large to call her beautiful. Her most endearing feature was her smile. She had a lovely generous smile, and she was a very smart young lady.

She didn't like school. It bored her, but she did well. It wasn't hard for her to pull off excellent grades. She'd even had her university of choice offer her an excellent tuition package for next year.

She smiled as she watched the installer slam the heavy, oak front door behind him as he left. The beveled windows, recessed into the thick wood, rattled. Really, she should have waited until Ruthie, their maid, showed him out. But he said he was busy so he showed himself out. She certainly wouldn't do that; and if he expected a tip, he wouldn't get it from her. After all, he was just doing his job.

She watched the dust motes chase each other in a sunbeam, filtered by the lace curtains on the windows and door of the entryway, for just a moment before she turned back to the telephone. The very first one in their neighborhood, and it was theirs.

She rubbed her hands together in anticipation. She was ready to enjoy this machine, device, or whatever the proper term people used. Her brother had told her all about it. He said he had already used one, said his friends had them. She didn't believe him. She knew he was a liar.

Her father had shaken his head in derision at the idea at first and her mother had said she didn't care, but all her friends at school had been talking about telephones for months. So she pushed and pushed until her parents agreed to order one.

Kate looked at a small piece of paper that had become crumpled in her hand. Setting the wrinkled document on the small table upon which the new telephone sat, she first smoothed it out, then picked up the receiver in preparation to dial. Bringing the receiver to her ear, she realized she couldn't place the call, there was someone else on the line.

"Hello, hello? Who's there? What are you doing on my telephone?" She couldn't understand why she heard someone else's voice and it was an unfamiliar voice.

"My dear, this is a party line. It seems we will be sharing the telephone. You may hang up now and try your call later," said a clipped woman's voice.

"When will you be done?"

"Really, some people's children don't have any manners. You may now leave, little girl."

Kate's face burned at the comments. This was going completely wrong. This was her telephone.

"Hi, Kate, what're you doing?" asked her brother as he entered the house, stopping to eye the new device. "Oh good, we finally got a telephone. Have you tried it yet?"

Her brother John was a tall, handsome young man who was struggling with his classes in college. He was five years older than Kate, with curly blond hair, and he was a natural athlete. When people saw the two of them together, most said, "Here come brains and good looks."

"Yeah, I was really looking forward to making my first phone call." She held out the piece of paper with Susan's number on it.

"Oh, are you going to call the Cooper place? Say hi to her brother Ron for me. Actually, ask him to call me about the big game tomorrow night. Thanks." He started to laugh, turned, and went up the grand staircase to his bedroom on the second floor.

Kate was so angry she started shaking. How dare John treat her like his secretary? She'd seen her father in his office and heard him talk to his secretary like that. "Take a letter, Miss Morris." There was no way she'd ever be that.

"Miss Kate, are you there? I just finished baking some carrot muffins, would you like one for your snack?"

Kate stood by the kitchen door. She wondered if Ruthie had heard the conversation between her and her brother. But Ruthie looked the same as normal, smiling at her. The maid turned to go back into the kitchen through the swinging door.

Kate could smell the muffins, making her stomach growl and her mouth salivate. *I am a little hungry*. Actually, this was perfect. She'd have her snack, then make her call.

She followed Ruthie into the kitchen. It only took her a few minutes to eat two muffins—they were delicious—then she went to the telephone again.

She pulled out the paper with the number, picked up the handle—there was a steady tone—and dialed the number. She started to giggle; it was ringing.

"Hello, this is the Cooper's residence."

Kate recognized the voice. It was Susan. It sounded just like her friend, only it was like she was speaking from far away. But she could easily hear her.

"Susan, this is Kate. Kate Baker. I'm sorry I didn't call you earlier, but the installer was late. We have a telephone now. Can you hear me?"

"Of course I can. What do you think of the telephone?"

"I can hardly wait to let everyone at school know that we have one. We're the first ones in our area."

"We've had one for a very long time—months, actually. All my friends at St. Pat's have one."

Kate could feel her teeth grinding together. Sometimes Susan was such a snob. They were friends from the riding academy her mother insisted Kate attend. She said it would help her daughter to meet the *right* people.

Kate heard a click and a soft laugh. "Susan, is that you?"

"Oh, dear, the children are on the line again. Free the line, please?"

"We just got on." Kate stood tall and looked at the front door. "Perhaps you could free the line for us for a few minutes?"

"Really, I never." Another voice Kate didn't recognize was on the line. How could this be?

"Actually, I need do my homework, Kate. I'll see you tomorrow," said Susan. The line went click as Susan hung up at her end. Kate could hear the other women breathing. "Your turn now, time to hang up," said one of the women with a sigh of disgust.

Kate slowly put down the receiver in the cradle. All she wanted to do was to have a telephone so that her friends could come over and use it.

She didn't have many friends. But that wouldn't work if other people were always on the telephone.

She looked at the telephone and slowly picked it up, making sure she covered the part she spoke into.

Smiling to herself, she heard two women talking about all kinds of things, personal things about their children, husbands, and their friends.

The more she listened, the more she was convinced that one of them was Mrs. Thomson. She had a daughter in Kate's class. Mary was nice, but shy. Kate wondered if this was the right family.

That would mean Kate wasn't the first in her school to have a telephone. This was horrible, everything was ruined, and it was Mary's fault. All Kate's planning, getting her father to do what she wanted, was for nothing.

Kate could feel her stomach start to twist and her jaw clench. She forced herself to take a deep breath and look at the situation calmly.

First, she wasn't sure if this was Mrs. Thomson. That's the first thing. Tomorrow she would go to school and talk to Mary to see if they had a telephone. Mary seemed nice. She had been in Kate's riding class, but stopped a couple of months ago. That's when Kate started thinking maybe she would stop riding too. Horses were big beasts that stank and defecated everywhere. Truth be told, even after all these years they still scared her.

Kate's jaw relaxed as she thought this situation through. First things first.

Looking at the telephone in her hand, she smiled. So far she had listened for a while and no one suspected she was listening. She wondered if she could do the same to other people and what secrets she'd hear.

Kate smiled to herself. Secrets. She loved secrets.

***

Kate stood in the hallway with the telephone tucked up under her ear, listening to one conversation after the other. It was late afternoon, the sun was setting, and the foyer was getting dark. She switched from one leg to the other. Her back was aching, and she wished Ruthie would come in and light the candles on the entry table.

She thought she had the Coopers on the party line; as least, it sounded like Mrs. Cooper. The more she listened, though, she realized it was a different woman. They were talking about dull topics: bunions, what to make for dinner tomorrow, the college game this evening, someone's unexpected pregnancy.

She was going to go and get a chair from the dining room to sit down on. Yes, that would be ideal; then she would be comfortable and could drink water while she listened.

The front door opened and her parents walked in. Kate studied her parents. At least they appeared to be in good moods. Her mother was laughing at something her father was saying.

"Really, Dorothy, we do need to do some more traveling overseas. The children are getting older. Soon we'll have two in college." Her father took her mother's coat and hung it in the closet beside his own.

"Tell you what, darling. I agree with you, but as for the destination, you and I have very different ideas as to what a *holiday* is. If John's team wins tonight, I get to pick the next holiday. If the other team wins, you get to pick. Fair?" Her mother laughed as she leaned forward and kissed her father on the lips.

"Oh, come on. Really, in public?" Kate's face grew warm with embarrassment. Her parents turned to look at her.

"Kate, we didn't see you there. This is our own home, thank you. How is your homework coming?"

Her mother responded to Kate, but was still looking at her father. "The big game is on this evening and we all have to go and support your brother. There might even be scouts, or whatever they're called, in the audience."

Kate, took a deep breath. *Oh no, I have a school project due on Monday.* It was a big one. She'd intended to start immediately after getting home. There was way too much work to do on it in the two days remaining of the weekend. Especially since she had a riding event all day on Saturday.

"Kate, what's the problem?"

"Mom, Dad, I forgot about my homework and I have a riding event all day tomorrow. I…"

"Are you saying you aren't going to your only brother's biggest game of the year because you forgot to do an assignment? Something you should have been working on for weeks?" Her father glared at her. He was angry; a vein in his neck throbbed.

Kate swallowed and took a deep breath. "Mother, I know you've said riding is good for me. That I would make the *right kind* of friends, but that hasn't happened. I've tried, but I'm just not the kind of person that has hundreds of friends. I do have friends, girls I've known for years, true friends, not just acquaintances. I would very much like to drop my riding lessons. I feel I know enough after five years to go for a casual ride. Please say yes. I really don't like horses all that much. And I would have more time to focus on my studies."

Her parents looked at Kate in alarm. "Are your grades in trouble?" asked her father, his eyes fixed on her, making her feel like she should squirm.

"No, they're fine. My grades are good, but I want them to be the best they can be."

Kate stopped speaking; her timing was really off in getting out of those stinky riding lessons, which she hoped to do really soon anyway. She knew if she said any more, they would ask more questions. She just needed the time for her project. She had already decided on the topic and done the research.

"We'll talk about it and let you know after dinner. But you *will* be coming to watch your brother's game this evening with the entire Baker family." Her father made his pronouncement, then he and her mother turned to head up the staircase.

Kate closed her eyes in relief. When she opened them, she smiled to herself, then quickly found an arm chair from the dining room. She placed it next to the telephone. Sitting comfortably now, she picked up the receiver again, making sure she covered the mouthpiece, pressing the other end to her ear.

This time she was right; this time she knew she had the Cooper's line. It was Ron talking to someone, a man with a very deep, distinct voice. "All right. Are you sure this is going to work?" The sound of Ron speaking was as clear as if he was standing beside her.

"If not, then he may have an accident. You wouldn't want that, would you? Because we'll make it look like you did it. I'm sure it would ruin both your lives. You understand, boy?" The last few words were said with a growl, sending shivers up Kate spine. The hair on her neck rose.

She waited until both parties disconnected before she hung up. Her heart thudded hard in her chest, her mouth was dry. *What should I do? Who should I tell?*

What did she actually know? Was it actually Ron Cooper? And who were the friends they were talking about? Could it be her brother John? He was the top scorer on his team, but it's only a game.

A silly college basketball game as far as she was concerned.

Whatever they were talking about sounded serious. She began to shake.

"Dinner's ready; everyone hurry, please." Her mother's voice echoed down the hallway.

Kate realized it had gotten very late. The candles on the table in the foyer were lit; it was dark outside. Soon they would be going to the game. She had to do something quickly.

Dinner was a slow affair, with five courses.

Kate sat listening politely to the conversation around her, nodding appropriately when there were pauses in the conversation or she heard her name mentioned.

Her mind raced with the telephone conversation she had heard. She wasn't at all sure of what it meant. She couldn't really identify the two speakers, although she could make a guess at one. But she knew so little.

"All right, then, everyone get into the car. We don't wish to be late," Father said as he rose from the table.

Kate knew John had gone ahead to school to warm up before the game. The Coopers had come to pick him up. As she'd looked out the window, she had watched Ron in the car thump John on the back as he took his seat. Ron was grinning like a madman.

Kate's stomach knotted with fear. She didn't know what to do. Before he left, she almost spoke to John to tell him what she'd overheard. Then she realized the questions he would ask, and the answers she didn't want to give would make her appear foolish, so she didn't talk to him. Now she wouldn't see him again until after the game.

No, she couldn't admit to anyone she had gotten this information from listening into a private conversation on their party line. *How horrible*. She was really a truly horrible person. But she had to try to keep John safe; he was her brother. If something happened to him and she didn't warn him, she'd regret it all her life. *Oh, I'm being torn apart.*

They arrived early at the school in her father's Oldsmobile, finding parking without difficulty. They went into the gymnasium and quickly found good seats, then settled down to wait for the game to start. *Maybe I should tell Mother or Father what I overheard? No, that would be worse than talking to John.* She clenched her hands together on her lap and kept trying to swallow, although her mouth was bone dry.

"Katie. Katie, I need to talk to you." A soft voice called from behind her.

Looking around, she spotted Mary waving to her. Her friend sat a couple of rows above them in the bleachers. Kate nodded, then looked to her mother seated next to her.

"Mother, Mary is here. I'd like to go and sit with her so we can talk." She made her eyes go a little bigger than normal and pasted what she hoped was an eager smile on her face. At least she hoped she appeared eager and not deranged.

"Certainly, dear, go and talk to your friend. Mary is a very nice girl." Her mother smiled and nodded.

Kate joined Mary, watching people streaming in. The gym was getting very noisy.

"Kate, I'm an awful person, but I have to warn someone in your family. I think I overheard two people talking about the game and what would happen to John if Ron didn't throw it," Mary said in a quick rush of words.

"Where did you hear that?"

Mary's face blushed a deep red and she looked down at the floor. She looked up at Kate with resolve in her eyes. "I know it was wrong, but I was listening in on our party line."

Kate smiled as she grabbed Mary and hugged her hard.

"Oh, Mary, that's wonderful!"

Mary slowly shook her head, looking at Kate with confusion in her eyes.

"Come on, let's go tell my mom and dad. I'm awful, too. I didn't know what to do. We must have heard the same conversation. With both of us hearing the same thing, we can tell my parents and not sound crazy. Believe me, my father will make it right."

Behind them Kate heard the band start the school pep song.

"Hurry, we have to hurry. Come on, Mary," Kate took Mary's hand in hers and dragged her to where her parents were seated.

"Mother, Father we need to talk to you both." Kate stood in front of her parents.

"Please sit down. The game is going to start," said a tall, gravelly-voiced man behind them.

Kate's heart squeezed hard in her chest and she gasped. She recognized that voice.

"Girls, please sit down; we can have a nice talk after the game." Her mother waved Kate and Mary to seats beside them.

"No. This is important. Very, very important."

Kate watched her father reach out to take her mother's hand in his and nodded to her. They both stood and left their spots as they followed the girls out.

Kate and Mary gave a quick summary of what they each overheard and how they had come by this knowledge.

"Father, we have to let John know before the game starts." Kate started to turn.

"You're right, but I'll do it," said her father. You and Mary go with Mother back to our seats. I see a friend of mine over there and I'm sure we'll get this straightened out quickly."

Kate looked to where her father was looking and spotted her Uncle Sam, a captain with the Vancouver Police Department. She looked at her mother, who nodded to both of the girls.

"Father, you can also tell him I think that one of the men I overheard is Ron Cooper, the other man is the tall man with the gruff voice sitting behind us who told us to sit down."

Kate and Mary followed her mother back to their seats.

When they were seated again, her mother whispered to her so as not to disturb those around them. "You did a good thing bringing this matter to our attention, even though it's rude to listen in on other people's conversations. But a good warning is still a good warning. It's all right, Father will take care of this. John will be fine." Mother smiled at Kate, softening her words, but the meaning was clear to Kate, something she would take to heart.

No more listening in on people's conversations, but she supposed *accidents* will continue to happen on occasion.

The teams came out and the game began.

Finally Kate saw her father climbing the stairs to their seats. He nodded and smiled at her as he sat down.

Then she noticed Uncle Sam walk up the bleachers until he came to the man with the deep, gravelly voice. Uncle Sam looked grave as he tapped the man on the shoulder and motioned that he follow him. Next, Kate saw her Uncle Sam and the man walking out of the gymnasium together. The man was wearing handcuffs behind his back.

The tension in Kate relaxed as the knot in her stomach eased. She soon began to enjoy the game. She cheered and Mary did as well.

John's team won the game. Mother immediately started talking to her father about making plans where Father would take her for a vacation.

As they left the gym, the crowd pressed around them while Kate held back to talk to Mary.

"I just wanted to say thank you, Mary. If you hadn't come forward to…" Kate stopped when she thought of John and what might have happened. A shiver ran up her spine.

"You're welcome, Kate."

"Mary, maybe we could do something else together? If you like to read, I've got a great selection of mysteries. It seems we have a few things in common, besides listening in on party lines."

Spirit Inn

Sarah wants to start a new life and a new cooking school, only the Spirit Inn has other ideas.

SARAH STOOD SHIVERING in front of the Spirit Inn, their new home. The cold was forcing her to lick her lips as she gazed at the Inn. Thankfully, in Bright Water, Oregon, a town of twenty thousand on the West Coast, it seldom got this cold in March—at least not for very long.

The Inn wasn't the prettiest place she'd ever been in or seen, but oh, the potential. There was so much potential, and it was hers. Actually, it was her and her sister Irene's potential.

The wind was fresh with the scents of salt and seaweed from the ocean and aromatic pine from the surrounding forest.

The building was a two-story, weathered wood structure, with wooden siding painted sage green, dark brown shutters, and an old coat of white paint on the trim. There was a long, wide, wooden veranda leading to oak-and-glass double front doors.

It was bigger than she remembered it, and it had been only two weeks ago that they had walked through the whole property.

It had been a grand home when it was first built over one hundred years ago, and it had gone through various conversions: hotels, motels, and names.

The property was located on the top of a hill but had no view.

At the back of the main building was a small, self-contained, two-bedroom cottage she and her five-year-old daughter, Nelly, would share.

Sarah was excited. She wanted to get inside the main house, look around, and then get set up in the cottage. She wanted to start making it into a real home for her and Nelly.

She smelled the sweet scent of lavender. It was so strong she could taste it on her lips. She licked her lips again as she looked down at Nelly, who was holding up a sprig of lavender she had just picked from a bush next to them.

"For me?" asked Sarah as she took the lavender.

Nelly looked up at her, her bright blue eyes happy and excited. Her soft blonde curls were bobbing. The blonde curls were a gift from her father, and her small nose and elfin chin were much like Sarah's. She was starting to bounce on her toes, trying to contain her excitement.

Sarah took the offered sprig as a gust of wind pulled it from her grasp, and like unseen fingers, braided her hair and the lavender sprig together. She thought she heard soft, gentle laughter in the wind.

"Pretty lady," said Nelly, her blue eyes twinkling.

Sarah looked around and there was no one there besides her older sister Irene, herself, and Nelly. She must be referring to Irene, a tall, slender woman with shoulder-length, dark-brown hair shot with silver, a woman in her late forties. Her eyes were a deep green hazel and often mirrored her emotions.

Outside on either side of the wide, cobblestone driveway leading up to the Inn were rows of cabins—twelve in all, six on either side, each a separate "room" with its own bedroom, sitting room, bath, and small, galley-style kitchen with a microwave, coffee maker, fridge, Formica counters, and cabinets containing dishes and cutlery enough for four people.

Surrounded on three sides by tall spruce and maple trees, the main house appeared solid. At least, that's what the realtor had said: that it was a solid building with a generously equipped, working kitchen, dining room, and twelve fully furnished bedrooms in the main building. They had checked it out as well as they possibly could for women who knew nothing about buildings, especially hotels or motels. They would need to learn how to maintain the place, but she was confident that they could learn as they went.

All Sarah knew was that it was theirs and she had to make this work. It was the only chance she had to provide a comfortable home and education for Nelly.

Being a thirty-six-year-old widowed mom with only a high school diploma and a few community college courses didn't give her many options, especially if she wanted to stay in her home town of Bright Water.

She and Irene had agreed to an equal partnership on this venture. She had the cooking and baking experience, while Irene provided the seed money. Sarah still couldn't believe how little this place had cost them; they'd gotten it for a song. They even had money for some minor improvements like painting and some new kitchen equipment right away.

"Mom, can we go in? Can we go in right now?" whispered Nelly in her loudest inside voice.

"Of course, baby. Are you ready?" Sarah asked Nelly.

Next to Sarah stood Irene, who was bankrolling this venture. Sarah waited for Irene's reaction to the little girl's enthusiasm. She didn't want to dampen Nelly's excitement, so she pulled the neck of her old, dark green parka tightly around her as she took a deep breath.

"Okay, let's go. Irene, do you have the key?" asked Sarah as she stepped forward to the front door of the building. She did her best to keep her hands from shaking. She didn't want Nelly to see how scared she was.

Sarah had a plan, a vision, and it was a big one.

First, they would open up the kitchen and restaurant while renting the rooms in the main building. As the money started to come in, they'd start updating the outside cabin rooms. The idea was to have the cabin rooms ready to rent out to students of their cooking school by this September. She had wanted to have the school open the following year, but Irene said no, they could do it all in six months. This meant they had to start immediately.

Sarah said she wanted six students as a trial, then they could test out the recipes she had been working on and collecting for the last few years. She explained to Irene that she wanted to prepare the recipes in the actual kitchen with real students as their six guinea pigs to test the recipes again, to *foolproof* them. Also serving the dishes at a discount to paying guests to help spread the word about the restaurant and the cooking school.

"Hurry up. Aren't you interested in seeing the new business? We have to get to work right away," said Irene in a stern voice as she stepped forward with the keys in her hand.

Sarah frowned at Irene's tone and attitude. Yes, this was a business, but it was their home, too.

They entered the Inn and the warm, polished oak front counter, walls, and ceiling greeted them. Sarah walked up and slapped the brass bell on the counter. It gave out a very cheerful ringing tone. She smiled at Nelly.

Along with the buildings, the Inn came fully furnished. Again, they couldn't believe their luck.

Even if they could only use a good portion of the equipment and furniture, they'd really be ahead of the game. Then they could take their time and go through the rest and refurbish things as they went along.

"Let's check out the rooms on this floor. I think they're to the left of the lobby down the hall," said Irene as she led the way. "You'll be wanting to take your pick from these rooms, I would think, so you're close to the kitchen. Of course, I'll take the cottage."

"You said Nelly and I would have the cottage," said Sarah as she came to a complete halt.

"I did, but I need my privacy."

"Fine, but you don't need two bedrooms, we do. The other rooms are all one bedroom and a sitting room at best. Besides, I was thinking you might want the rooms on the top floor next to the covered, glassed-in deck. We could make it into a private solarium for you and your plants. We could make it very private; we could even build a wall across the hallway and then put two units together. You'd have your own kitchen. It would be even bigger than the cottage," said Sarah gently, pushing her temper back as it started to rise.

Sarah calmed herself. She'd had a sneaking suspicion bossy Irene would try something like this and was ready, knowing her sister's love of her privacy, plants, and sunlight.

She'd also make sure that once they finished the tour, she would grab some of her and Nelly's things and start moving into the cabin right away. As they say, possession is nine-tenth of the law—or in this case, ownership.

"Hmm, maybe that would work," said Irene, her brow wrinkling in thought. "We'll check it out. Let's go to the dining room, or should I say, the future restaurant."

Irene led the way, turning on the lights down the short hall, with its broken tile flooring and mud-colored walls, into a large, dark room. She turned the lights on and they saw a room with warm pine panels and a high ceiling painted a soft blue.

On the left as they entered was a double, varnished-oak-and-brass door. Sarah pushed it open to discover a sheltered side garden full of dappled sunshine on this cloudy day. She stepped outside and Nelly followed behind her.

There was a nice, wide, stone pathway leading through the garden until it split into two paths, one going left to the parking lot behind the cabins until it split again, one part becoming a path that wandered until it disappeared into the trees. The other wide path led to the right and after fifty feet, she could see a fence and gate and a tiny portion of the siding of a modest, gray house tucked behind a few laurel and rhododendron bushes. That must be the cottage she and Nelly would call home.

Bubbles of excitement welled up in her chest. This Inn was going to be hard work, but it would be worth it in the end. She'd have her own cooking school and be a part owner of an Inn.

"Oh, look, have you ever seen such tall rosemary bushes? Look, I think those are hardy fuchsias; they're dormant right now, but in the spring they'll bloom. What a wonderful place to put an herb garden. I can see green onions, sage, lavender, and pots and pots of thyme and all kinds of mint," said Sarah to Nelly, who was standing next to her.

There seemed to be a long, deep, satisfied sigh on the wind as she spoke and she looked down at Nelly, who had her head cocked and was listening very intently.

"Mom, did you hear that? Was it the lady again?"

"Sarah get in here, you can look at your silly plants later," scolded Irene as she turned and marched back into the Inn.

"Yes, honey, I heard the wind in the trees. Let's go." Sarah turned her attention on her sister and went back into the large, warm, dining room.

"Fine, this looks workable. Let's go see the kitchen and determine how much space and equipment we have to work with," said Irene as she again led the way until they entered the kitchen.

Upon seeing the size of the kitchen, Sarah's heart sank. "Oh, dear. Is this right? I don't remember it being so *small*," she said.

Nelly, who stopped at her mothers words, looked up at her mother, her blue eyes wide with concern.

Sarah and Irene looked around, carefully taking in the large, double stainless steel sinks, the old, cracked, grey and red floor tile, the grill over a large double oven, and the six-burner stove with another oven underneath. There was a large refrigerator and an eight-by-four-foot butcher block counter, with a narrow metal stand and clips for orders. There was a large, dingy window over the sink, and the walls were painted a spring green that had gone grey. It was dark. She looked up and realized that at least half of the fluorescents were not working.

A lot of this, she knew, could easily be taken care of—the cosmetic stuff and a good, thorough cleaning would do wonders. It looked like the kitchen hadn't been used in years.

"Okay, I think we'll need to plan how we're going to teach and work in this space. I was hoping we could have individual stations, like they have in, hmm… schools," finished Sarah weakly as she looked at Irene. "I don't really remember this configuration."

"Mom, come look what I found," said Nelly as she peeked around the corner going into another room.

She skipped over to her mother and took her hand; she was so much like Sarah that Sarah had to smile.

"All right, you little imp. Let's see what you found," Sarah said, as she followed Nelly behind what she had thought was an exit.

Irene continued talking to herself about the uses of the space as she saw it. "Well, that's fine. I was going to talk to you about the school anyway. I think we should delay it for a couple of years. We'll start with renting the upstairs rooms, then the outside units, and maybe open up the bar, and then, if we need to, the dining room..."

A sudden loud clatter and a fierce, freezing gust of wind funneled through the kitchen, blowing Sarah's straight, shoulder-length, strawberry blonde hair softly around her shoulders. She glanced behind her at Irene and saw that her sister's face was white and her dark brown hair was being twisted around her head.

They heard a loud groan of someone in pain as the temperature in the kitchen turned icy cold.

"Lady, no. Don't be mad," said little Nelly as she came to stand next to Sarah and look up at the ceiling.

Sarah realized the back door wasn't open. What was happening? Maybe she *had* heard voices when she thought it was the wind; and this cold, swirling wind was really strange. Her mind jumped to the word *ghost,* but she pushed it away. She knew there were no such things as ghosts.

"No, Irene, we bought this Inn for a cooking school; otherwise I wouldn't be here. We need to talk about this later this evening," she said as she looked behind the wall at what her daughter had discovered. Why did Irene pick now to fight? They had settled all this before they bought the place. This time she wouldn't let Irene win just to avoid an argument. This time she would make her stick to what they had agreed on.

The wind stopped suddenly and the temperature of the room returned to normal.

Sarah saw shelves and shelves of pots and pans, a lot more of them on the floor, and dishes that seemed as if they were all still where they had been stacked on their separate shelves on the far wall.

The area was large—a good twelve-by-twelve space. "Irene, come and look at this. Nelly found a lot of really good things. I just found another stove, another fridge, and a walk-in freezer in here, too. All commercial grade. I think we're right on track with my school."

Irene approached Sarah and Nelly, who were standing together looking at everything they had found. Irene glared at them, her lips pressed together; first at one, then the other.

"I think we found the other third of the kitchen," said Sarah to her sister. "I'll take the measurements tomorrow and draft a floor plan. I think if we have three good-sized stations, we could at least start with six students and do our test kitchen by January; it will give us more time to prepare rather than September."

"No, we'll make this into the Inn it's supposed to be," Irene said with a stubborn tone to her voice. "Then we'll see about the other. I've changed my mind about the cooking school."

Sarah shivered as she noticed the room get colder again, like an exterior door was open.

She saw Irene's lips form a thin line as she clenched her jaw. Sarah knew she was in for a fight with her sister.

"The plan was for a combination of my dream of a cooking school and your dream of owning an Inn. What's happening to everything we talked about and agreed to?"

"I changed my mind," said Irene with a smug tone, "and since I put up the money for this venture, I get to call the shots."

"You said we were equal partners." Sarah stopped to glance at Nelly, who was watching them.

Nelly's eyes were filling with tears as she looked from her mother to her aunt. She had been traumatized by the sudden death of her father, a year ago—they had both been—and they were just now starting to heal.

Sarah had to make her daughter her priority. "Tell you what, Nelly, why don't we go together and start to unpack the car. We'll get some of our things out and then go for a bite to eat. Let's get the beds and the kitchen set up. Okay?" said Sarah as she turned to leave.

"I haven't made up my mind about the cabin," snapped Irene.

"I have," said Sarah as she stopped and stood tall and straight with her head up.

She was so angry she was shaking, but she had to hide it. The best thing right now was for her to keep busy.

"Sure, Mom," said the little girl as she ran from the kitchen, through the dinning room, down the hall, and out through the antique oak wood-framed glass front doors.

"We'll talk later. I suggest that we sleep on it. I will do up a draft floor plan so we can look at it tomorrow," Sarah said before she turned and followed Nelly without waiting for a reply from Irene.

She couldn't understand what was happening. They had discussed this all beforehand. It had been settled, but it seemed that her sister decided to change everything they'd agreed to now.

There was no way Sarah would have quit her bank job to come to work as a cook and housekeeper for her sister. That was not going to happen.

Spirit Inn

As Sarah exited the Inn through the front doors, all the lights suddenly went out.

* * *

Nelly and Sarah were laughing as they moved their car and parked it behind the cabins. They gathered some of their things and walked together up the path to the cottage. Sarah pushed open the gate and then walked up to the front door of their new home. She unlocked the door to the cottage with the shiny brass key Irene had given her. It was her's now and she was going to keep it.

"Are you ready?" she asked the little girl standing by her side, with her arms full of bags and bears.

"Come on, Mom, let's go. I want to pick out my room," Nelly said with an impish grin.

Sarah chuckled. "We know which room is your room. Okay, let's go and take a look at the place, but remember we can change the colors, and once our stuff is in, it will look a lot different."

"Yeah, I know, Mom: clean and paint. Moose and Rocky want a bed."

Sarah opened the door and let Nelly rush in first. They had already seen the cottage, and like everything else at the Spirit Inn, it had a lot of possibility.

Nelly shrieked with joy as she ran through the front room and dropped her bears in the smaller of the two bedrooms. Sarah could hear her chatting to someone, probably one or both of her bears. She'd always had a very good imagination.

Nelly rushed out, opened her arms wide, and did a twirl around and around until she got dizzy and fell to the glossy, hardwood floor in the cozy living-room-dining-room combination.

124

It was equipped with a floral patterned, badly sagging sofa and a red upholstered arm chair, arranged in front of a red brick fireplace, and a round oak dining table, with four mismatched, worn oak chairs surrounding it.

The place had a musty smell, wrinkling her nose. She coughed as the dust invaded her mouth and nose. Sarah was sure they would find all kinds of issues, from spiders and mice to leaky roofs, but she was prepared to tackle one problem at a time.

The windows were dirty and there were spiderwebs in every corner, but there was also a nice hooked rug in the middle of the living room floor. In the center of the room was a solid oak coffee table, and it matched the end table next to the arm chair. The floor looked like it was made of solid oak planks. Sarah knew it would all look lovely once it was cleaned, and she could hardly wait to start.

Sarah went into what would be her bedroom to drop a pile of clothes and linens onto the old-fashioned brass bed.

"Where have you been!" Irene strode into their home, her features angry, her cheeks flushed crimson. "I've looked all over the place for you. We have a real problem. We have no power in the Inn. This is a disaster."

Sarah reached over to flick the light switch on one wall of the bedroom. The light in the ceiling went on. "It seems to be fine in here, and it was working in the main building earlier. Have you checked the breakers and the fuses?"

"How do I check them? I've always lived in apartments; I don't know about breakers," said Irene in a very curt, angry voice.

"Well, maybe we need to learn about things like that. After all, you said that we don't want to hire a handyman right away. We have other things we need to do. Let me get another load from my car and then I'll be right there."

Sarah turned to face Irene, who appeared to have calmed down.

Sarah felt a tickle on the back of her neck. She looked around to see if there was anything like cobwebs to cause it. There wasn't.

She looked down and saw Nelly on the floor by her feet, grinning up at her; she covered her mouth with her hand as if she was keeping herself from laughing.

"Go on, Irene. I'll grab a flashlight from the car and meet you in the kitchen. If it were me, I'd put the electrical panel on the wall behind the kitchen. Come on, Nelly, let's go find out what the problem is."

Irene went back to the Inn as Sarah and Nelly quickly went to their poor old blue Toyota Camry to grab another load of boxes and clothing from the back seat. They had sold almost everything they had except for their clothing, a few pieces that had special memories, and some pictures.

Once back at the cottage, they dropped everything on the living room couch. Sarah wondered how long she could live with the old rose-printed fabric. Oh, well, she could always toss a blanket over it.

She picked up the flashlight she had brought from the car and left the front door open to help air out the cottage. As they walked along the path to the gate, in her mind she could see the possible future. She could smell roses and flowers in her front yard and hear the soft drone of bees as they gathered pollen from the lavenders and the birds singing in the trees. She hugged herself to make sure that this was real.

It was.

Then she heard a terrified shriek coming from the top floor of the Inn. Oh, Lord, it was Irene. Sarah ran through the garden to the dining room door, pulled it open, then ran down the hallway and raced up the winding oak staircase.

At the top, she ran down another hallway and then into one of the rooms at the end of the hall next to the sunroom.

"Irene, Irene! Are you all right?" Sarah yelled from the open doorway.

"There's no need to shout!" Irene yelled. "The windows are open. The entire neighborhood can hear you."

"I gather you're fine, then? What happened? Did you see a spider or a mouse?" Sarah stepped into the dusty, grimy, sitting room and then into the bathroom that connected the bedroom and sitting room together. It smelled of stale air and acrid cleaning compounds.

She started to laugh as she saw Irene, sitting in a tub overflowing with bubbles and water. "You've got a lot of bubbles there, Irene. Why are you having a bath now, in the middle of the day?"

The warm water and the sweet-scented bubbles lent a warm, festive air to the second floor of the Inn. She was temped to catch some in her hands and blow on them.

"Bubbles, Mom, can I have bubbles, too?" asked Nelly as she entered the bathroom and did what Sarah wanted to. She started blowing the bubbles around the room. They were on the counter, in the sink and toilet, and on the tiled floor.

Sarah ended up having them on her lips and tongue. She laughed as she watched Nelly play.

"I was testing out the tub to see if it was long enough and if I would like this room, then slipped and fell, trying to get out. The water won't turn off. The handle just goes around and around. We'll have to turn off the water at the main water valve. Please turn it off as quickly as you can, before we have a major flood. I think the key is on my key ring, and I saw a small shed next to the back door of the kitchen that might be the utility room," said Irene.

Sarah saw that Irene was fighting back tears and knew she was vulnerable. "Good plan, Sis. I'll run downstairs and take Nelly with me. We'll check out the utility room and turn off the water. I'll yell up in a few minutes. Let me know if it works. Okay?"

"Sure. I'll try and get up again and mop up this mess." Irene smiled weakly at Sarah and then at Nelly. "Well, at least the floor in here will be clean. Once you turn off the water, you might be able to find the breaker for the power in there, too."

"Good thinking. Nelly, go into the other room while I give Aunt Irene a hand," Sarah took a deep breath, smiled at her sister as she held out her hand, and helped Irene up and handed her a towel.

Sarah dried her hand, then took Nelly's hand in hers before going downstairs and outside.

Soon the water was turned off and the lights were turned on.

Sarah and Nelly hurried back upstairs to see how Irene was doing.

"Oh, Mom, there's the lady. Isn't she pretty?"

Sarah's attention was drawn to the large living room of the second floor, with its worn, sagging, mismatched sofas and chairs and the scarred wooden coffee tables and end tables. The sofas and chairs sagged so badly they looked like they could eat people. She wondered what stories the sofas could tell.

She looked around the room but didn't see anyone. "Isn't who pretty? Come on, honey, we need to find Aunt Irene and see how she's doing." Sarah went toward Irene's sitting room.

She froze when the sound of a woman's singing met her ears as she went down the hall. She smiled as she recognized it. The song was an old Irish lullaby she used to sing for Nelly. It was taught to her by her husband Nick's grandmother. She hadn't heard the song in years.

"Irene, ready or not, here we come," she called out to her sister, letting her know they were back.

"In here," Irene responded, calling from her sitting room.

Sarah looked at Nelly before they walked hand in hand into the room. It was clean and sparkling. The accumulated dust seemed to have vanished.

She looked at her sister, who was dressed in comfortable slacks and a blue sweater that accented her blue eyes and cool skin color.

"Wow, this looks great. How did you do it so quickly?"

"I don't know. I just started in the bathroom, did one thing at a time, and soon the bathroom was done. I opened the windows in my bedroom and was going to start in here, too. But I came in after putting some clothes away and it looked like this."

Sarah looked around at the room. The sofa and chairs were all tidy, there was a beautiful, antique quilt on a quilt holder in the corner. A large, mahogany-framed picture of a young, beautiful lady in a full-length white-and-pink dress, long blonde ringlets, and an elfin face with bright blue eyes hung over the desk. She walked up and admired the painting and read the small brass plaque on the bottom. It was beautiful.

"Well, whatever you did, the place looks great and so do you. What was in that bubble bath you had anyway, a magic youth potion?"

"Very funny, but thank you. I guess we'll have to call the plumber tomorrow and get the tub fixed and the water on. Oh, there's something I forgot to mention to you. I've arranged for a few people to join us for dinner on Friday. I was thinking you could make your wonderful shepherd's pie or a lasagna?" Irene looked embarrassed as she sat down and gave Sarah a weak smile.

Sarah looked at her sister and sat down on the couch beside her. "Nelly, can you go and play down the hall in the upstairs living room for a little while? I'll be right here."

Sarah looked at Irene; her eyes sparked in anger.

Irene's eyes were in her lap and she started to play with her engagement ring. She had worn the ring every day since her fiancé's disappearance five years ago. She waited for him to return. "Look, I'm sorry for the way I'm behaving, Sarah, but I'm really scared. I've put everything I have into this place. I'm forty-seven years old, and if this flops, the odds of me making a lot of money are slim and none. This has to work—it's my retirement fund."

"Irene, we need each other, just like we discussed. I know you're worried; so am I. This is my and Nelly's future, too. I need a good safe place to raise her and want a great education for her and this is the only way it's going to happen."

Irene nodded as she listened to Sarah.

"But we need to be partners—you with your administration skills, me with my cooking skills. Together, the Spirit Inn will be a fabulous cooking school and Inn. We just need a little time to get things done. Which Friday were you thinking of for the dinner?" Sarah already suspected what the answer was, but hoped she was wrong.

"Ummm… this Friday, in four days? I invited about twenty-five people. Can we make it work?" Irene gazed at Sarah with hope in her eyes.

Sarah bit her lower lip as a knot that had formed in her stomach loosened. Fighting with her sister, she hated; but this she could do and enjoy. She nodded. "I'll need your help getting the kitchen cleaned and stocked. Then as I start on the sauces, you'll have to work on the restaurant and bathrooms. Deal?"

Irene nodded, then continued, "We need to talk about the division of duties and flow of work. By the way, I hired a very nice man as our manager, and his wife is going to help with the dinning room and the cleaning. They'll be living in the first cabin; it's a two bedroom, Number one."

"Then we won't have twelve units for the students?" asked Sarah, frowning at her sister.

"We will. The end cabin, number twelve, is a two bedroom as well, and we can offer a discount for the shared accommodations."

"Good plan. So we're back to an equal partnership?" asked Sarah.

"Mom, meet Beth. She lives here, too," said Nelly, re-entering the bedroom. She was holding up her little right hand, her fingers curled as if she was holding on to someone's hand.

Irene looked at Sarah and shook her head.

"Don't you see her?" asked Sarah in a very soft voice, looking up above Nelly's shoulder.

The room got cooler.

"What are you talking about?" asked Irene, looking confused.

"Do you see the painting over your desk?" asked Nelly.

"Yes, it's beautiful," said Irene.

"Is that whose hand you're holding, Elizabeth Clarkson's?" asked Sarah as she looked at the picture.

Nelly nodded and grinned at her mother and aunt, then looked up at her new friend.

"Well, it seems that we have another partner, a silent partner—a ghost named Elizabeth, or Beth," said Sarah as she nodded with understanding and glanced at the name on the bottom of the painting.

"That explains a lot of things. Welcome to Spirit Inn, indeed," said Irene as she looked at the painting, then at Nelly and at Sarah.

"To our new home, the Spirit Inn," said Nelly as she beamed at her aunt, her mother, and her new friend.

One For All

Metamorphosis can be scary but sometimes it can be exhilarating.

I FLUFFED THE pillows on my bed and quickly straightened my ocean-blue down comforter. I walked across the hardwood floor and pulled back the white, lined curtains over my desk. The desk had been my grandmother's and I took good care of it. I loved the feel of the smooth, glossy wood under my fingers.

My room has light blue walls that match my eyes; white, lined curtains; and the ceiling and trim are white. Against the far wall, there is a blue-and-white covered love seat with a cozy, cream-and-white fleece blanket. It really adds warmth and hominess; also, it is my favorite place to read.

I smiled at a little ruby-throated hummingbird sitting on the feeder outside my window. It was beautiful, with its bright, black eyes and long, slender beak, light green head, bright red, iridescent throat (the color spread down and across its chest), then bright green-blue shoulders and back, with a soft grey underbelly.

The bird flitted away a few feet, looked at me, and then came back and sat at the feeder again. I stood there and watched for a few moments.

I always felt happy when I saw them. They really lifted up my spirits; there was just something about them. They were fast and feisty.

I had read that they were the bird that the Aztec warriors used as their totem. Not only were they fast, but also they were agile fighters who defended their territory with an incredible fierceness.

I wasn't sure if I should have a quick shower, dress, and then have breakfast like normal...my stomach growled loudly in the silence. Nope, I had to eat first.

I could smell toast and coffee coming from the kitchen; I started to salivate.

I grabbed my thick, purple robe and slipped it over my rose-pink fleece nightgown. I finger-combed my shoulder-length blonde hair and tucked it behind my ears as I opened my glossy white bedroom door. I peeked out of my room to see if I was alone. I slowed before I reached the kitchen. I finished belting my robe, then entered.

I had already heard my parents talking and my younger brother Scott whining about his breakfast. Why were they talking so loudly? Scott had run out of his gross, chocolaty cereal and had to eat something a little healthier. Poor baby.

They all stopped talking and turned to look at me. I smiled first at Mom, a tall, slender, pretty woman, with dark blonde hair and a touch of makeup to subtly accent her large blue eyes and full lips. Next I saw Dad, or Professor Jacksen, as his students called him, a gentle man of medium height, dark complexion, and warm brown eyes, who sat with his toast and coffee at the kitchen table near my brother Scott. Scott looked up at me from his cereal. He was eleven years old and looked like Dad, with his brown eyes and hair. They were all dressed and finishing off their breakfast.

"What?" I asked, trying to smile at them when all I wanted was to grab a couple of pieces of toast slathered in peanut butter.

The room was bright and warm.

The cabinets were done in warm wood tones with clean, gray, granite countertops and a blended travertine floor. The granite was great; you could spill stuff on it and it didn't really show and it was easy to clean. So if you missed a few spots, Mom never saw them.

"Jewel, where are your glasses?" asked my Dad as he picked up a piece of toast and took a large, crunchy bite.

I wanted to walk up to him and grab a piece of toast off his plate.

"Jewel, why are you here?" asked my mother. "It looks like you haven't showered or dressed. Unless you're wearing your jammies and robe to school?" she said, trying to be funny.

"Glasses upstairs," I said to my dad. "I'm really hungry and just want something to eat before I take a shower," I explained to my mom.

I popped a couple of pieces of rye bread into the four-slice toaster, then added another two before I pushed down the handle to start the toaster. Then I waited and waited. I kept looking at the toaster. What was wrong with it? It was taking forever. Finally it popped. I scooped up the four slices of toast, grabbed the peanut butter, a knife, an apple, and a banana, and ran back to my room.

My heart was beating so fast I could barely hear the separate beats. Hungry, very, very hungry, must eat now.

I closed the door behind me, jumped on the bed—I didn't care about the crumbs—and really wished, for the hundredth time, that I had a lock. Mom and Dad had been so overprotective since this spring. The elementary school gym had been struck by lightening three times. Our class of grade sevens had been the only ones there—and our teacher, of course—but we were all fine. No one had been hurt and now we'd all moved up to high school. In Vancouver, B.C., we went from elementary school in grade seven right into high school in grade eight. That was the scary thing, high school.

135

Going from knowing where everything is and everyone's name to not having a clue and feeling lost, totally lost. I didn't even know where all the bathrooms were.

I could hear footsteps coming up the stairs and down the hall toward my room. *Here comes Mom.* I could hear her in my mind, already getting angry. I could sense her feelings. As she got closer and I focused on her, I could actually hear what she was thinking. She had enough to do today at work without me acting stranger than normal. Her thoughts kept going from me to work, then back to me again. Okay, I didn't want to hear my mom's thoughts. Way to much information. This was really scary and unexpected. I looked out the window and started to think of hummingbirds. Good, it was working, I couldn't hear her anymore.

I just wanted to eat in peace, then get ready to go to school. I had enough problems with being in a new school and grade eight. Yeah, it was exiting, nerve-racking, scary, and everything else. The older boys were great, but the tests were a lot harder.

My door opened and there was Mom. She put a stiff smile on her face—it didn't look normal or reach her eyes—as she looked at me.

"Yes, Mom? Look, I'm fine. Just a little hungry. I'm fine, really." I know that I spoke really fast, way too fast. My heart was beating hard against my chest. I needed to get Mom out of my room and get to my food.

"Okay. As long as you're sure," Mom said, still looking at me, or looking me over from head to toe.

I sat waiting, willing her to leave.

I took a deep breath and deliberately spoke slower. "I'm sure. I'm good. I was just hungry. Like you say, I'm a growing girl."

I hoped the bit about being a growing girl would please her.

I was just over fourteen and small for my age, and I knew that she was really worried that I wasn't growing properly.

Mom nodded slowly. I could tell she really wanted to feel my forehead to check if I had a fever, but she was trying not to baby me.

"I'll be down in a minute."

She nodded, gave me an uncertain smile, turned, and left.

"Close the door, please, Mom," I said. I finally heard her footsteps going down the stairs. Her mind was focused on her work again.

I grabbed the first piece of toast, ripped it in half, then stuffed the entire half into my mouth and chewed. I started to choke and caught my breath. *Boy, it's dry*. I slathered peanut butter on another piece, ripped it in half, stuffed both pieces in my mouth, chewed, and swallowed. Soon all my toast was gone. If Mom could see me, she would be horrified. That certainly was not the way I had been taught to eat, as if I had no manners at all.

After I finished breakfast, I ran across the hardwood floored hallway into the bathroom, locked the door, and downed two glasses of water. Then I wiped my wet, crumby, peanut butter mouth with the back of my hand.

The bathroom was a good-size family bathroom, but only Scott and I shared it. It had walls the color of cream, soft green tiles edged by translucent brown glass tiles, and white fixtures. It was cozy, clean, and functional.

My stomach stopped growling. Finally I felt a little better, more human.

I ran the water in the sink and brushed my teeth. I purposefully didn't look at myself in the mirror. There was a droning in the room. I listened; it sounded like the *Flight of the Bumblebee*. Suddenly it stopped and I realized the sound was coming from me.

Oh, please, please let this not be happening to me.

My stomach started doing flip-flops. I looked at my hand; my fingers were strange. They were long and very thin. I still wouldn't look at my face, I was too frightened.

I remember the day it had happened clearly. The day of the storm.

We were still in elementary school, in the gym. It's a large room, with a high ceiling and cement block walls, painted a light yellow. It had a small stage on one side, basketball hoops on two sides, and patterns for games on the grey floor.

It was late spring, just this last March. We had been told by the teachers not to look at the sun because there were massive sun flares that were supposed to happen. Only it wasn't sunny at all, it was pouring rain in the afternoon and we had a huge thunder and lightning storm. Our gym had been hit three times by bolts of lightning. Each time the lightning struck, it came through the neon lights, down the metal practice climbing wall, and spiked into the floor. Some of it went to the bleachers, too, but that was a smaller amount. The air around us sizzled. You could feel the power of the lightning all around us.

We laughed at the girls with really long hair because their hair floated up around them like a cloud. One of the kids even said that maybe we'd all turn into superheroes.

We all laughed.

But I remember thinking maybe he was right. After all, we had what they called a trifecta in horse racing when you had three winners: massive sunspots, lightning bolts, and we were all going through puberty.

I looked back at my hands. My nails were growing, very thin, black, and long.

Please, not me. I don't want to be a freak. That's what I heard someone say in the high school yesterday: that we had changed into freaks.

Not me, not everyone was changing. Right? There had been about twenty-five students in the gym that day and only about ten had changed. Where were the ones that had? No one would tell us where they had gone. We couldn't even visit or see them.

Maybe this was only temporary and things would go back to normal.

There were still a good half the class that nothing had happened to. Even my two best friends, Darlene Drake and Paula Bell, were still unchanged.

I turned, pulled off my robe and nightgown, and started the shower.

If I refused to acknowledge it, then it wouldn't happen. I held onto the belief that not everyone who had been in the gym when it happened would change.

I jumped into the shower, ran around under the water and between the streams of water, and was finished in a few seconds. I wasn't very tall, or big. About five feet tall, about one hundred pounds, and small boned. They call it petite. I still held out hope that I would grow four or five inches. After all, I had just turned fourteen, and some girls still grow after that. I used to be teased all the time, being called Gidget the Midget. But they stopped laughing after I took some self defense classes in both Karate and Tai Chi.

I remember in elementary school when I flipped a really big guy over the fence onto the soft grass. Everyone suddenly had a new respect for me. I was so shocked after I tossed the guy that my heart almost stopped. It was all I could do not to run up to him and make sure he was okay.

But he landed well, rolled, and jumped up with a big smile on his face, wanting me to do it again.

I dried off and put my towel back on the rack. I took a deep breath, slowed my heart rate, and prepared myself. I knew I had to look at my face and see if it had changed.

I slowly looked in the mirror. I started with my eyes. Well, they had turned from a light, summer-sky-blue to a shiny, intense black; I couldn't see any of the whites of my eyes at all. I had always had a heart-shaped face; it was still the same, only more exaggerated and pointed. It almost looked as if my original smallish nose had grown longer and sharper, like a long, pointed, bird beak.

I stepped back as I took a deep breath. *Oh, my gosh!* I looked at the rest of myself. I could never have imagined this in a million years. It looked like I was dressed from head to toe in a humanoid costume of feathers. Soft, short feathers. Even the coloring was similar to my little ruby-throated hummingbirds. The brilliant, iridescent-scarlet throat and chest, with green on the head, wings, and back, and a soft grey underbelly.

I was really pretty!

No wings, but anyone who saw me would know what I was. I knew what my new name was: Iridescent Feather, or Feather for short. Yup, that was my name and it felt right.

I was scared, but I needed to find out what else I could do besides sense emotions and read minds.

I laughed and went up on my toes, lifted off the floor to hover for a second or two, then slowly sank back down. Oh, what fun. I experimented and took a little hop and stayed up for a short while. I thought of going down and relaxed my shoulders and dropped down to the floor.

I looked into my black eyes in the mirror. *This can't be happening*. It was a dream. I closed my eyes, lifted my hand, and slapped myself hard across the face. *Ouch*. I slowly opened my eyes. *Sill a hummer*. Then I lifted my hand. My fingers were now long and slender and had long, thin, black fingernails. I pinched myself hard. *Nope, still a hummer*.

I had been terrified about changing. But I thought it was cool that I was a hummingbird. I took a small hop. *Ouch!* I hit my head on the ceiling. *Oh, man, I can fly!* Wow, how cool was that! I started to laugh. *It's so exciting*.

I floated back down and realized I was suddenly a little hungry again; not ravenous like before, but enough so I'd grab something to eat on the way to school. I wondered if, with my new talent, I would be burning a lot of energy or calories.

Maybe, if I did something as a hummer, I'd have to refuel. I know that birds go through an incredible amount of food to keep their little wings and bodies going. *I guess our grocery bills are going to get higher*.

"Jewel, Mom says you need to get out of the bathroom. We've been calling you for twenty minutes. I've got to brush my teeth. They want to leave soon. We need to hurry," called Scott through the bathroom door.

"Oh, crumb! Okay, I'll be right out. Why don't you go into your bedroom and get your shoes, jacket, and books ready?"

"Fine."

I heard him leave. *Little brat*.

I heard him muttering that his teeth were fine and he didn't really need to brush them again. Then I heard him think that he had brushed them a couple of days ago and that was fine. Mom would freak if she knew; they always made us brush at least twice a day.

I'm going to save that information for later; it just might come in handy.

After I heard him close the door of his room, I grabbed my robe, threw it over my shoulder, picked up my nightgown, and ran to my room across the hall. Then I slammed my door shut.

"Okay, Scott, the bathroom is yours."

I dropped my robe and nightgown and stood in front of the full-length mirror that was attached to the back of my bedroom door.

Okay, I had a few minutes to master turning and turn myself back again. No problem. I was really nervous. Okay, I'd take my mind off it. First, I'd pick out what I was going to wear today as I figured out how to do it.

I closed my eyes and thought *human*. I tried to remember what my body felt like before. I opened my eyes. Nothing, still a bird.

I opened my closet. Maybe I shouldn't go to school today. That might work, but only for a very short while. Besides, I really wanted to see my friends. I really needed to see them. Maybe they had changed too, maybe they hadn't. Maybe I was all alone now. Maybe they would take me away, too? No, this is my home and my family. My eyes filled with tears as I pulled out a pair of black leggings and my favorite red top.

No, don't go there. Somehow I knew then I wasn't the only one who had changed.

I tried to be positive, happy, and imagined myself running along the sidewalk, remembering how it felt as my feet hit the pavement and as I lengthened my stride, taking in deep breaths, running faster.

I opened my eyes. Nothing.

I looked at the family picture on my desk. I really looked at myself. I closed my eyes and thought of the picture. I felt something start to change.

I peeked, my eyes opened a little, my breath caught in my throat. I was changing. I looked at the picture, saw my smiling face and the rest of my body. I focused and built a picture of me in my mind. I rubbed my fingers together; my long talons were gone. I opened my eyes. My body was back to normal. I wasn't a bird any longer!

"Yes! Halleluiah!" I yelled and got changed into my clothes as quickly as possible. Then I checked my eyes. They were still black, but they looked more like human eyes. That's fine—so I was wearing cool contacts instead of my glasses. I could handle that.

I smiled for the first time that morning as I slipped on my shoes, grabbed my jacket and backpack, and headed for the front door.

I checked the clock in the hallway before I left the house. My best friend Darlene should be leaving from our usual meeting place. Normally, I'd just jog the four blocks to meet Darlene. But I didn't want to trigger another change.

I had recently been told, by a popular grade twelve girl, that *real* girls don't run down the street like an elementary school kid. I started taking long, loose, ground-eating strides down our side street to Fraser Street, then on to David Henderson High, my new school, hoping I'd catch up to Darlene along the way.

The day was already hot. The sunshine bounced off the cars parked on our side street and warmed the sidewalk. I quickly passed the tall, ornamental cherry trees on the boulevard and the church on the corner with its high, slender tower and simple brass cross.

I was now on the corner of Fraser and had four blocks to go to get to Forty-Ninth Avenue, then seven more to the high school. The traffic was busy, noisy, and stank with all the buses and cars, although rush hour was over. There were people on both sides of the street, crowding the sidewalk.

I made good time.

I saw Darlene just before she crossed Forty-Ninth Avenue.

"Hey, Darlene!" I yelled, hoping she'd hear me. She did and turned around. Darlene was a fourteen-year-old girl with short dark hair, a pear-shaped figure, and a round face, with beautiful, dark brown eyes and a very quick mind.

"Where were you this morning?" she asked as I caught up with her on the other side of the road.

"Oh, you know, I have a brother that messes around and then suddenly needs the bathroom," I answered. I looked at her very carefully to see if there was anything different about her. If I couldn't see anything, should I tell her about me? I really didn't know. I had been trying to think of something all the way here. Do I trust her? Yeah, of course I do. With most things, anyway. But with everything? I'd say yes, but something also tells me to be very cautious with everyone, even my own parents. Just in case they want to do something that's good for me I don't agree with.

Dar slowed a little and I slowed as well. She quickly glanced at me. "Yeah, I have a sister, remember? What's with the eyes? New contacts?"

"Yeah, just got them. What do you think?" It wasn't a lie, it was the truth—I did just get them, but they weren't exactly contact lenses.

"They're different." She nodded. "I like them. Are they hard?"

"I guess so. It's just what they gave me," I said as I picked up the pace. I didn't want to be late and I wanted to catch up with Paula before lunch in case she needed anything. Darlene seemed to be fine so far.

"How are you doing?" I asked in a soft voice. There was something about Dar that wasn't normal. Maybe I was projecting me changing onto her and hoping she had changed, too.

144

"Good. Yeah, really good. Um, have you heard about some of the other kids that were in the gym at Oliver?" she asked in a gentle tone. She looked at me from the corner of her eye and I nodded.

"What's happening, anyway?"

"I don't really know, but I heard that some of them are changing, they have superpowers, you know, like in those comic books I lent you?" Dar asked looking ahead down the street.

"You mean like flying and running superfast?"

"Yeah. How about you? Anything?" asked Dar.

I slowed and stopped. Dar slowed as well, but avoided looking at me. I waited. I could feel confusion coming from her.

Should I tell her or not? Can I trust her?

"It's okay, Dar, you can call me Feather," I took a deep breath and answered her truthfully.

Dar stopped and turned to me. Her eyes were normal. Then she blinked and I saw that her eyes had changed. They were like cat's eyes, a deep golden color with a vertical pupil. I could sense her nervousness.

"Cool. Very nice. Do you have a tail?" I complemented her and smiled at her when I asked my question.

"Never mind."

"All the time or sometimes? Oh, do you have one now?" I asked as I looked at the back of her skirt.

"Never mind, but you can call me Kat. That's with a *k,* not a *c*."

"Okay, let's drop it for now. Have you told anyone else? When did it happen? Do you know how to control your powers? Do you know what they are?" I asked in a rush. I felt bad about asking all these questions, but the more I knew, the more I could help other people. That was my story and I was sticking to it.

145

"I haven't told anyone. I overheard my mom and dad talking last night. They said people are scared of us. I'm really scared, too. I don't want to be something people are going to study. I don't know how to control what I have, and I really don't know everything I can do. You?"

"No. I haven't told anyone, either. I just started to learn about what I can do this morning. I just got really lucky and figured out how to change back to looking like me before I had to leave for school. I almost got caught by my folks and Scott. The little blabbermouth. Let's talk to Paula at lunch and see how she's doing?"

Dar nodded and we picked up the pace again. We heard the first bell ring and hurried to class.

For the rest of the morning, I sat in my classes and thought about the changes we were going through. The more I thought, the more I realized we needed to find a safe place to try out our new gifts or talents. Someplace where we could learn to control ourselves.

There was the gym at Oliver Elementary; the school board had closed it for testing since the lightning strikes. They wanted to make sure it met with all the safety regulations. There was an empty church across from Darlene's place; it was for sale. But neither of them seemed very good places to test our powers. We had to have a place that, if we damaged it, no one would care.

I could hardly wait to talk to Paula. I looked up at the classroom clock. Time was really dragging this morning. I wanted to get going. I wanted to try my hand at changing and flying and to see what other gifts I had.

Finally the lunch bell rang and everyone in my science class grabbed their books and hurried out as the teacher announced a surprise test for tomorrow, first period. I tried not to rush.

I strode down the hallway, jogged down the stairs, down another long hallway, and into the cafeteria. It smelt like old cooking grease, French fries, and vinegar.

Dar and Paula were already there and had saved seats. The cafeteria was a huge, dark, and dingy room that reminded me of a cavern. The ceiling was high, but the lights were weak. There was little decoration and the beige walls and grey floors went well with the hard, beige picnic-table-style tables with attached benches to create a very depressing area.

Paula was the third member of our little group. She must have had her hair cut—boy, was it short. She was a little on the round side, but because she had warm, brown, curly hair and a round face and big glasses, she could carry it off. The lenses in her glasses made her dark brown eyes looked huge and her eyelashes looked long and thick. At least they usually did, but today her eyes were a deep emerald green. I looked carefully at Paula and saw that her eyes didn't look large or magnified, they looked like a normal person. That could only mean that her lenses had been changed to regular glass. Interesting.

We liked the image of the Three Musketeers, one for all and all for one, only we were girls; but the rest worked for us.

My heart was beating hard and fast and getting faster. I decided I better sit down and take some deep breaths. I still wasn't sure how this transformation thing worked and I didn't want to turn into a hummingbird in the school cafeteria in front of everyone.

"Hi, all," I said as I sat down.

"Hi, long time no see. What's new with you?" asked Paula.

"I need help with science. We're having a surprise test tomorrow. A surprise to us, since we don't know what's it's about," I told the girls.

"I can give you a hand," said Paula.

"Is there an easier way rather than studying all night? The answers to the test might be nice," I said jokingly.

"Who do you have, Gilroy? I heard he never changes his tests. My sister had him two years ago and she has all her tests and notes. Just saying," answered Paula with a slight shrug.

"Thanks. But I'm afraid I'm going to have to do it the old-fashioned way and learn it. I've never cheated on a test yet, and I don't want to wreck my perfect record now. Just joking. No, it's wrong. But thanks, anyway." I looked at both of them and we all started to laugh.

Yeah, I knew we were all a bunch of good girls—or nerds—and proud of it.

"Is there somewhere we can go and talk privately?" I asked in a loud voice so they could hear me over the din of about a thousand voices talking all at once. We have a good-sized high school.

"Actually, if we sit closely together and talk normally, no one would hear what we're saying over this noise," said Paula. She was brilliant and excelled in botany. She was planning to become either a professor or a researcher.

I look at the other two. We all sat closer and leaned forward a little.

"Paula, how are you feeling?" I asked. I may as well open up the conversation with a new topic.

"Good, you?"

I could sense her emotional confusion and uncertainty, but no direct thoughts.

"What do you think of my eyes?" I asked, shifting to look directly at her. The lights weren't the best in the cafeteria, but I hoped she could see them.

"Oh, nice," she said as she glanced at me and reached for her milk. She smiled, nodded, and something soft slid across the top of my hand.

I was proud of myself when I didn't scream. I slowly looked down and saw the tendrils of a plant. It had pretty, hot pink flowers. And then I felt a little scratching as something was drawn across my fingers. There were sharp, long thorns amongst the flowers and leaves.

I looked at Paula. "What's your name?"

"I'm Vine. You're?" she asked as she looked between Darlene and me.

"I'm Iridescent Feather, or Feather for short, hummingbird, and our friend is Kat with a *k*, not a *c*," I answered for both of us.

"Interesting. What now?" asked Paula.

"I think we need to find a place where we can experiment and learn how to use our powers." I drew in a steadying breath, not realizing I was actually nervous. "So, does anyone know a place that would be large enough so we can jump, fly, test our strength and out our gifts? I've thought about the empty church across from you, Dar, and the gym at Oliver, but I don't think either are very good. Any other ideas?"

Darlene shook her head, then glanced at Paula, then me. I could sense the emotional uncertainty coming from all of us.

"Actually, my uncle has a barn. It's in the city, not very far from where we live. I bet we could use it. It's very big and high. He was building and storing ships in it, so it should do the trick. What do you think?" asked Paula.

I waited for Darlene to speak. I had led this meeting enough already. I looked at her and nodded.

"Well, um, could we trust him? I mean, he wouldn't turn us in, would he?" asked Darlene as she steepled her fingers.

"We can trust him. His son is Gunter. He was in our gym class, too, and he's already been taken away. My uncle won't talk to anyone about us," replied Paula in a firm voice.

I nodded. "Good. Those are exactly the people—the kids, our friends who have been taken—I really want to find and help. But first we need to find out how to deal with ourselves, then find out where they're being held. How do you all feel?"

"I think this is a good start. But…" Darlene paused.

Paula finished the thought for Darlene "Yeah, it's a start, but it's not going to be easy or fast. This is the start of something new for us. And for the world."

I agreed. As much as I was itching to learn about being a hummingbird, this was very serious stuff. If we got caught, who knew the full consequences? We certainly didn't. But we had a chance to help our friends, and hopefully other people, too. Exciting and scary times lay ahead. But I knew that together we could make a difference.

My friends looked at me, their eyes determined and bright. "How do we stand?"

We all nodded. We reached across the table, put our right hands in on top of one another's, and said in unison,

"One for all, and all for one."

Rebellion

A new job on a new world. Too bad the timing wasn't right.

"Hi, I'm Erin. You must be Tony," I said when a man approached wearing the uniform of the International Border and Immigration Service.

This was the first time we had actually met although we had been in touch by electronic mail.

I turned and looked up at Earth. The dome wasn't completely clear, as I had thought it would be. It was tinted a bronze color, probably to filter out some of the sun's more deadly rays. It was amazing, seeing Earth hanging in the ink-black sky like a big, blue-and-white ball.

"Good guess. I'm Tony Eland; it's nice to meet you. You're Erin Thorne, I believe?" he said.

I nodded and we walked side by side into Elliot Space Station's warehouse district. I smelled the cold wet of the cement, and the grease and oil from the equipment and forklifts. There was also a hint of a pine scent, reminiscent of wooden shipping crates.

There were a dozen self-contained domes on the moon. They were all pressurized and included artificial gravity—close to Earth normal—air, and fresh water from the reclamation system augmenting the water mines on the dark side of the moon.

This dome was for the mining and processing of minerals that would be shipped to Earth.

Suddenly shots rang out around us, forcing me to dive for cover, my heart racing. With the first shots, I dropped on the cement floor, rolled onto my belly, and sighted my pistol over the shoulder of Tony Eland, the man I was replacing on my moon assignment. I tightened my fingers around the smooth, hard grip of the gun and fired in the direction the shots had come from.

Interesting, the gun handled differently in the moon's low gravity even though the domes had earth normal gravity: the kick wasn't as hard, but the bullet also didn't stay up as long and the trajectory was different. It was most likely her bullets, a specialized hard plastic that could kill a person but would not penetrate the dome.

My heart started to pound and my mouth went dry as adrenalin flooded my system.

I smelled the acrid stench of fresh gunpowder, mingling with a damp mustiness coming from the warehouse.

The bullets pinged off the wooden crates and the metal barrels stacked around them in this massive warehouse. The building was twice the length of one of Earth's football fields and a good three stories high. Bright lights hung from open metal scaffolding overhead, illumining the warehouse and its contents.

We were in the new warehouse area under a new dome next to a new space station, Elliot Space Station, so luckily everything around us was pressurized.

Huge crates—a few wood, but mostly metal—full of goods surrounded us. Some consumer soft goods, some perishables, and some commercial goods that were destined to be components of homes and businesses; at least, that's what the shipping manifests said.

Another shot pinged above our heads. We both ducked and lay flat on the cold, dirty, greasy, cement floor.

"I'm going to get closer, cover me," I said to Tony.

He crawled closer toward me.

"What did you say, Erin?" asked the tall, dark man. Tony's head was shaved, but on his upper lip was a thick, neatly trimmed mustache. His black pants and light blue shirt with the International Border and Immigration Service flash on both shoulders were clean and pressed. He obviously took pride in his appearance.

My uniform looked just like Tony's, only his fit better since he was a lean, six-foot male that the uniform had been designed for. The color was good for me; the blue was nice and suited my red hair. But I really hated trying to fit my five-feet-eight medium female body, curves and all, into a man's shirt and pants. It just didn't work.

"I said this isn't fair. This assignment was supposed to be like playing a round of golf, a walk in the park, a beautiful lunar vacation. So far, this has been a really lousy vacation." I crouched low and ran across the slippery cement floor.

Shots started and echoed in the large area. I tasted bile as the acid in my stomach tried to escape.

"A vacation? Where did you get that idea?" asked Tony in a loud voice as he rolled and came up next to a large metal barrel. He crouched and looked around the corner of the barrel to see where the shooters were hiding.

Everything went suddenly quiet.

Too quiet.

"The guy at the International Border Guard Recruitment Center on Earth told me this new station would be a piece of cake, like being on a holiday. I figured it would be a good first assignment for me."

I heard someone coming toward me. It sounded like heavy, size-fourteen work boots hitting the cement floor. Much like my ex-boyfriend's boots.

I dove, rolled over my shoulder, came up behind a medium, four-foot-high wooden crate, and fired in the direction of size fourteen.

"You did identify us when you went into the foreman's office, right?" I asked as I took a second to glance around.

"I didn't go to the foreman's office. I thought you did. I just got here and met you at the door," said Tony as he squeezed off another couple of shots toward the sounds of the footsteps.

We heard something land with a thud on the cement.

"Do you think we should identify ourselves now?" I asked. Tony was the senior member of the team; I was waiting for him to take the lead.

I had been told by the Elliot Space Station people that he, Officer Eland, had been here for the last fifteen years while the station was built and knew who everybody was and where everything was kept.

"This is International Customs and Immigrations. Drop you weapons," yelled Tony. There was a shot punctuating the end of his sentence. As I watched, I saw Tony disappear behind a crate and not come up.

There was a massive barrage of gunfire. It sounded like it was coming from at least two different directions, but it was hard to tell.

"Do we know who these guys are?" I asked as a bullet whizzed close by my head. I flattened myself against the crate.

"No," answered Tony through clenched teeth. It sounded as if he were still to my right.

"Ah, you let them know that we were going to be working in here today?" I asked as I moved toward his hiding spot.

"No. I usually just walk over, say "hi" to whoever is working on the floor, and do my business. This is driving me nuts!" yelled Tony as the barrage of bullets increased, making conversation impossible.

I got to his side—he was on his butt, leaning against a crate—and knelt down. I saw that he had a wound on the top of his shoulder. It was bleeding. I motioned him to show me his arm and he shook his head. Then he handed me a strip of cloth that looked like it had come from the bottom of his shirt. I tied it over his wound, then kissed my fingertips and touched the wound lightly.

"You'll be fine," I said softly, smiling at him.

He nodded at me. "Thanks."

"Okay, fellas, that's enough. You're in an enclosed dome. You have no place to run to and nowhere to hide. Give yourselves up," yelled Tony.

I quickly went back to my previous hiding place and waited for the next round of gunfire.

"I left a…" I started to say. Then I saw a red flash from the corner of my eye.

Next thing I knew, a tall, heavy-set man with a long, bushy beard came out from the six-foot-high metal drums with a long wrench raised in his hand. He was staring at me with anger and hatred.

I turned, karate-chopped his arm. The man grunted and dropped his weapon. It clattered on the cement as I kicked it away.

"Sir, face down, on the ground, now!" I commanded as I watched the man lie on the ground. I can't help but be polite, that how I was trained.

"Okay. Everyone, I have a loaded gun pointed at your friend's head. I need you all to come out and drop your weapons. Then we can talk about what's happening," I said as I tried to hold my gun steady and keep my hand from trembling.

Nothing happened. No one moved. There wasn't a sound in the warehouse.

I put my best poker face on, waiting for whoever was there to do what I'd told them to, because I didn't know what to do next. Then I realized that Tony wasn't there with me. Oh, great. Was he okay? He was hurt, but it hadn't looked that bad. Or had he left?

"Hold on. We're coming out," said a low male voice. I heard a few pairs of boots shuffling closer to me in the warehouse.

"Stand where I can see you and drop your weapons." I thought I'd say it again. If it worked the first time, maybe it would keep on working.

I heard something or someone behind me.

I turned, my gun in my hand, ready to fire. The person behind held up his hands. He was a small, thin, scared-looking man in his midtwenties. His face was pale and his eyes were big and round.

What was happening in this place?

"Erin, I'm coming out," said Tony. He waited a moment, then stepped out from behind a wall of stacked boxes.

"Do you have cuffs? I don't have any yet."

"Yeah, that's nice. You just about blasted the boss." Tony looked at the young man standing there and smiled. "Hi, George, you can put your arms down now…"

"Oh, I didn't know," I said. What was going on here?

"Sam, are you okay?" asked Tony, calling to the other person, on the floor waiting to be cuffed.

"What is this, a joke?" I asked, feeling my temper start to rise as I figured it out. Not a nice trick. I hated practical jokers.

"Of course. You can't expect to come into a place like Elliot Space Station, which is all of six buildings and about one hundred and twenty people, and not expect a welcome of some sort," said Tony as he holstered his gun.

Tony reached into his shirt pocket and pulled out a small data pad. He keyed some information into it and then handed it to me.

"Before we go on, could you please sign this for me? It's just a simple release form. Please read it, sign it, and I'll send it to the boss. You'll get a copy for your records, too," he said, handing me the pad.

I looked at it. He was right, it was simple. It said that I had arrived on Elliot Space Station and was now starting my job as an International Customs and Immigration officer. It looked right, so I signed it.

I heard voices and looked up. There were a good dozen men, all different sizes, color, heights, and shapes, coming toward me. They were all wearing jeans and worn work shirts and they had one thing in common: they were all smiling. I got big hugs from some and pats on the back from others. Some had a lot of body odor and others smelled like cologne or a flower shop.

"Thank you. We're so glad you're here. Finally, we have something else to look at besides Tony's ugly mug," said one of the men, who sported interesting tattoos on his neck and had smelt very clean and nice.

"Come with me and I'll give you the low-down," said Tony as we left the warehouse.

"Oh, shouldn't you introduce me to the warehouse keeper and the guys?" I asked Tony.

"Sure. Guys, this is Officer Erin Thorne. She is my replacement," said Tony in a loud voice.

Together we briskly strode to a couple of what looked like golf carts a little way from the main warehouse.

"Okay, this will be your ride," said Tony as we stopped by a royal-blue golf cart with white top. It was a custom job since it had four seats and a short bed at the rear.

I slid into the passenger side of the open vehicle. I let Tony drive.

"This facility is approximately three miles wide by three miles long. So it isn't very big, but when you're in a hurry or have to carry something heavy, this should do the trick."

"Tony, when are you going to leave our fair little town?" asked a heavy man wearing a straw western hat and a blue plaid shirt. He had just pulled up by the door of the warehouse in another cart, only his was candy-apple red. He turned and looked at us.

"As soon as I can, Mitch, as soon as I can," Tony answered as he pushed a button and turned on our cart. We started backing up and heard an explosion behind us.

Startled, I took a deep breath, then look toward the sound; but I knew it was Mitch.

"That was Mitch, wasn't it?" asked Tony. Without looking at the smoking cart, he slapped our cart into park, slid out, and ran toward Mitch.

"Yes, it was," I said as I jumped out of the cart and rushed to Mitch, too.

I had a head start, but soon I was just looking at Tony's back. Man, could he run.

We arrived at the side of the smoking cart. I crouched down and waited as Tony felt Mitch's neck for a pulse. I saw Tony smile and shake his head.

"Okay, Mitch, hang in there. The boys will be here in a minute."

The sound of a siren split the air and soon another motorized cart appeared, only this one had an enclosed back and there was an International Red Cross symbol on the side.

Two guys dressed in light green surgical scrubs jumped out and ran toward us.

"He's got a pulse, it's steady. Amazing, but you know what they say about mean men. Anyway, George, Bill, this is your scene. If I don't see you before I leave, take care," said Tony to the men as he stood up.

I stood up, too, and stepped back.

Tony took a step forward and introduced me. "Oh, guys, this is Erin Thorn. Erin, the blond one is George, and the dark guy is Bill. Guys, be nice."

I shook my head, laughing as we walked away. Tony had a smile on his face.

"Okay, and now for the rest of the tour," I said.

"Oh, yeah, back to my script. We have six buildings in our dome, or town, and the Elliot Space Station. We have one ship a day. The ship lands in the morning, the flight you were on, and it leaves in the late afternoon, the flight that I will be on," he said as he slid into the cart.

I slid into the cart next to him and he backed up and then started forward.

"You just saw our warehouse. It's broken into two parts: international goods waiting for clearance, and domestic goods. The domestic goods are further split into two sections: goods awaiting exportation, and goods that have cleared and are waiting to be delivered. The entire facility is geared around mining and the support of that mining operation. Simple. Questions?" he asked.

I shook my head. So far so good.

"There are six buildings in our town—we use the term very loosely since there are only about one hundred and twenty people living here altogether. There are about twenty who work at the station itself, forty in the warehouse, and sixty miners. The biggest of the six buildings is the warehouse that you were kissing the floor of a few minutes ago. Then there's a large, long building called the Store. That's over there. It's the one painted forest green. It contains a coffee shop, restaurant, grocery store, post office, movie theater, clothing store, bookstore...you get the drift. Then you have four dry-mud-colored barracks, where everyone lives."

"Stop. That's not what the brochure said. The brochure said this was a growing and lively town with all the features of a large city. Then it described what you just listed, but no one said it was all in one building," I said.

I was horrified. *This can't be true.* Then I remembered Tony saying something about nine square miles. I'd thought he was joking or talking about the warehouse area, not the entire town.

There was no way on earth, or the moon, that I could live in something this tiny. There had to be more. Tony was again pulling my leg. He had to be. I could feel my heart start to beat harder. I looked around for a way out of this place. My mouth felt dry and my throat started to tighten.

"Of course that's what the brochure said. I wrote it. I've been here for fifteen years. The only way I can get off this rock is to have someone else come here and take this job. And you have, so I'm leaving," said Tony with a very smug smile on his face.

"What? No, absolutely not. I suffer from claustrophobia. I need to get out for a drive and to stretch my legs at least every second day, if not every day. They lied to me! Therefore, the contract is void. It wasn't valid."

We heard what sounded like a police siren. I looked down the road to see another cart, a black-and-white police logo painted on its side. I hoped the police were going to check up on what happened to Mitch.

"Is it always so lively here?"

"Actually, it's a slow day. There wasn't much cargo on the flight that you were on."

"Okay, now tell me, when are you really leaving? This afternoon? Why?"

He laughed as he glanced at me. "For pretty much the reasons that you don't want to stay here. The walls are closing in on me. I've been stuck on this rock for fifteen years. I've taken online courses and gotten degrees in accounting and law. I've gotten pretty good at online poker, too. By the way, the same restriction applies to you— the only way you can leave is to find a replacement, and that may take a while," he said and nodded to himself, gazing straight ahead.

We passed a second warehouse, the "Store," and I saw that it had different entrances and doors with names of different services.

I realized that I was indeed in a mess. What I had told Tony was the truth: I had a very bad case of cabin fever. I wasn't great in enclosed spaces. If I didn't get out of here, I would go downhill quickly. I could already feel my heart starting to pound and my hands getting damp with perspiration at the very thought that I was trapped. I noticed my breath was coming faster and faster.

"I'll figure out a way to get off this rock." I tried to take in deep, slow breaths, focusing on something else and not thinking that I was trapped in the small enclosure and would be for years and years and years. I felt like screaming.

"Up ahead is the barracks, as we fondly call it" Tony said in a flat voice.

I forced myself to listen to what he was saying. "Barracks? I thought I would have luxurious, state-of-the-art accommodations with spectacular scenery?"

"Yeah, me again. Maybe I can get a job writing ad copy. What do you think?" asked Tony.

I nodded. "I can control this. I can control this," I said to myself in a low voice. I was determined not to let my anxiety start a panic attack. That was something I'd never had and never wanted to experience. But I knew I had to get out of this place. I didn't care what I had to do. I was going to get out.

Tony stopped the cart in front of the barracks. I looked him. He met my eyes and he nodded. "You've really got it bad, don't you?"

I shook my head. I didn't want a stranger to see me like this. My eyes were dry and burning. I blinked, trying to get some relief. I even tried smiling. I stepped out of the cart. My legs were shaking but I forced myself to move and followed Tony into the long, low, mud-colored barracks set on a dusty, rock-and-sand-strewn field.

Oh man, the quarters were ugly and depressing. It would be merciful to blow it up and start again.

"Do you get involved with crimes, like what happened to Mitch?" I hoped at least my work would be interesting. But I knew that in a very short while I wouldn't be able to concentrate on anything except finding a way out. I sensed any attempt to do so could get very dangerous.

There was an explosion somewhere in the distance. It sounded similar to the one that injured Mitch.

"Come on. I'm just picking up some things and then I'll be checking out. The shuttle leaves in a couple of hours," said Tony as he opened the barracks' front glass door.

We walked down a long, dim corridor with wooden doors and brass number plates. We stopped in front of one of the doors and Tony opened it with an old-fashioned brass key.

"Tony, I'm sorry, but I can't stay here. I was hired under false pretenses. The company lied to me. Really, I can't stay here. Besides, I haven't even signed anything yet, except the document that you had me sign. Was that…" I stopped and looked at him.

Did he just screw me into being stuck here forever? I could feel myself getting angry. How could he have done that to me?

"No, Erin. What you need to sign is a contract with either Elliot Space Station or the International Border and Immigration Service. They are the ones that would hire you or let you go with a contract."

"I haven't done that and I don't have a contract. Does that help? I have to go back to Earth. Please." I hated the pleading tone in my voice. I'd rather be shooting, blowing things up, or chasing after bad guys. This was not like me at all.

"Yeah, you're not the only one," he said as he opened the door and we walked into his cramped, beige, one-room studio.

I looked at him. "Please. What do I need to do to get out of here?"

He sat down on the one plastic chair in the room and motioned that I should sit on the twin bed in the corner. I did.

"Do you have three million dollars?"

"Don't be stupid. If I had three million dollars, I wouldn't be trying to get a job." I shook my head, trying to figure what Tony was talking about.

"The three million is a one-way flight from the moon to Earth."

"But I don't have three million dollars. So it really is a nonstarter." I was trying to be logical.

I really didn't want to lie, cheat, or steal, but it seemed the company that hired me started it first. They lied. This may be the exception to my rule.

I heard another explosion. This blast, though small, was closer, maybe at the Store.

Tony seemed unfazed by the explosion. "That's fine. What kind of credit card do you have?"

"Why are there so many explosions? Tony, what is happening here?" I asked. I was getting a really horrible feeling that there was a major point missing.

"Never mind. I have Diamond Platinum; it will cover anything anywhere. I'll zip your ticket on my card, and when we get to Earth, I'll send the bill to Elliot Space Station. They'll have to cover it. And then I'll cancel my card. Good thing you haven't unpacked," said Tony, trying to smile.

He selected clothing from his closet and chest and put them next to me on the bed. He started folding them, putting them in a dark brown, leather duffel bag.

"Actually, I forgot to pick up my luggage at the space station."

Another blast, shaking the walls, showered us in fine dust. It seemed to be right outside the front door.

"What's happening here? Why do I get the feeling that we're all prisoners? That once you come here, you can never, ever leave? They don't pay you enough for a trip home and they don't hire people except on a need-to basis. You are stuck here forever, aren't you?"

Tony looked at me and nodded. "We have to go now. We'll drive to the spaceport. We can pick up your things."

"Tony, please tell me, what's with the explosions?"

"It's the workers. They've had enough of the treatment, the lies, and everything. They were shanghaied just as you were. It's happening. It's an all-out revolt. I was hoping the uprising would hold off for another couple of months, but since they attacked Mitch today with the small bomb, it's started. They won't do any damage to the dome, just all the buildings *in* the dome."

I looked out the window. Another blast went off. This one was at the far corner of the barracks. It seemed they were destroying the buildings, as Tony said, one by one.

"Come on. We have to go now," said Tony as he grabbed the duffel bag and swung it over his shoulder, along with a black leather briefcase.

I followed him down the hall and to the cart.

It didn't take long to get to the warehouse. Once we got there, I saw that chunks of the walls and sections of the roof had disappeared. Tony showed me where the tunnels were for the goods and passengers. We drove our cart all the way into the circular holding area and got off. I collected my luggage and everything went as planned.

We met with no resistance or even questions at the ticket office. The crew behind the counter was nervous and kept looking at each other. They just handed us our tickets and didn't even check my documents.

I went to the ladies' room and changed from my uniform; by the time I got out, the crew had all left.

Then I heard explosions again. Only this time they sounded different. Bigger. It sounded like they were being set off outside the dome.

I met Tony. "The bombs are getting closer. You don't think..." I started to ask, but stopped as he slowly shook his head.

"Come on, let's go," he said. "We're going to have to move as quickly as we can, right to the ship."

That's when I felt the cement pad that we were standing on rock. Some of the walls were starting to buckle and pictures were falling off the walls.

I looked at Tony. I couldn't believe it. Maybe getting stuck in a small town under a dome wasn't so bad after all. No, I knew I couldn't do it. Leaving was the only option.

"Follow me," said Tony as he lengthened his stride. I walked quickly next to him. I saw the signs to the gate we would use to depart.

There was an explosion right behind us as we passed the security station. I turned and saw there was a hole in the inner wall of the station building. People were screaming and the roof started to come down in chunks around us.

Tony looked at me, grabbed my case, and started to run. I put my purse over my shoulder and ran right next to him.

The intercom came on. "All passengers with tickets for the flight this afternoon at four o'clock go directly to the departure lounge. The ship will be departing early, within the next fifteen minutes. Please make your way directly to the departure lounge!"

The floor shook again, twice more. We ran faster. People were falling all around us, screaming. Some because of the explosions, but most were knocked down by other people.

We had to go over, around, or through the entangled bodies.

I lost my balance and was knocked to my knees but picked myself up and continued to run.

I was starting to run slower, breathing hard and gasping for air by the time we got to the walkway to the ship.

The announcer was urging all passengers to board as we reached the waiting lounge. The gate staff stood by the door and didn't look at our tickets, they just waved us through as quickly as possible. Their ashen faces and flitting eyes told me the situation was growing more desperate by the moment.

I grabbed two seats together by the window and Tony swung into the seat next to me.

I had just belted in when the captain announced the hatch was closing and to prepare for liftoff.

Looking around, I saw there were still a few empty seats, but the crew was closing the hatch. There were no safety announcements on this flight.

I could hear the warning blasts from the ship, signaling immediate departure. I looked at Tony and silently thanked him.

The ship started to rumble and shake as the engines warmed up. Soon I heard the metallic sound of the gantries holding the ship in place move away. Now was a critical point and I closed my eyes. The ship would make it into orbit or it would be destroyed, taking us with it.

Suddenly a burst of thrust from the rockets slammed me back in my seat. The rumble of the engines increased. Ignition. The pressure increased as I felt the surge of takeoff from the moon's surface. My mouth tasted dry and metallic, my breathing was rapid. Tony had gripped my hand and was squeezing it tightly.

I held my breath and closed my eyes for a few seconds.

There were no more announcements from the captain as I was pressed into the seat by an increase in gravity as the ship accelerated to escape velocity.

I relaxed as my heart rate slowed. We had left the gray pitted surface of the moon behind.

I'd made it. I had managed to live through a rebellion on the moon.

We were returning to Earth and I was never coming back to the moon again.

About the Author

Rita lives on the Sunshine Coast in British Columbia with Russ, her husband, who is also a fiction writer.

She has written for years and is an alumna of the Oregon Writers Network and the Greater Vancouver Chapter of the Romance Writers of America.

Her most recently published stories are Fire in Their Hearts with Russ Crossley, Ladies of the Jolly Roger, and Tales of the Fantastic all from 53rd Street Publishing.

Please visit her website at http://www.ritaschulz.com to view her other works.

Other titles you may enjoy

Short Fiction

Blarney
Flower & Bird
Party Central
Once Upon a Time
The Scarlet Curse
Spoken Words
The Brownie's Holiday
A Little Old Fashioned
In The Land of Dragons
A Little Kitchen Magic
Silver Light
For Pete's Sake
Cleaning Up is Hard to Do
Confessions of a Bold Maiden
All for One
Lucky List
A Spark of Courage
Party Line
Spoken Words
Spirit Inn
One For All
Graybill
Rebellion
The Prize

Collections

Ladies of the Jolly Roger with Russ Crossley
Ten Tempting Tales with R.S. Meger
The Fantastic Five with R.S. Meger

A title from 53rd Street Publishing you may also enjoy.

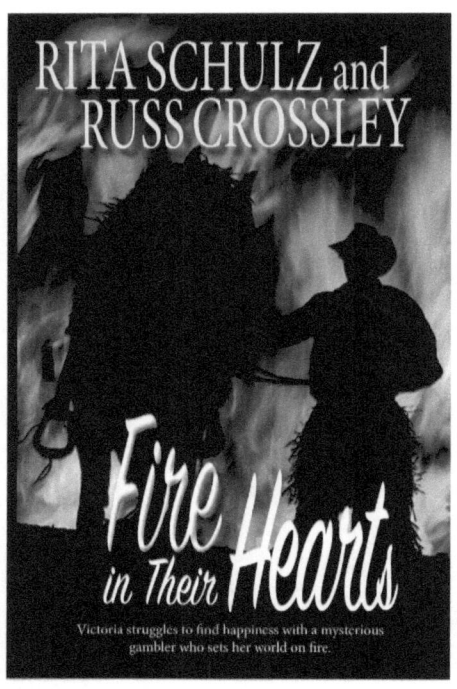

Vancouver. 1886. Within 24 hours a deadly fire will sweep the town.

When mysterious gambler, Tyler Scott saves Victoria Ann McNichol's life together they find themselves thrust into a world of the unknown, a world of love, passion, and intrigue neither expected.

The two lovers worlds collide when the frontier explodes in violence, betrayal, and murder forcing Victoria and Tyler to join forces against incredible odds.

They will either survive to their happy ending, or die trying.

A new romance by Russ Crossley, author of Zomopolis, Antique Virgin and My Zombie Prince, and Rita Schulz author of Ladies of the Jolly Roger.

This title is available in ebook from your favorite online retailer and may be ordered in paperback from your favorite bookseller.

www.ingramcontent.com/pod-product-compliance
Lightning Source LLC
Chambersburg PA
CBHW020248130626
46549CB00005B/2116